Jet Journey

The world of flying is always exciting — even more so when you know what is going on. So read on and discover why planes stay up in the air and how pilots find their way through the sky. There's a plane spotter's guide and a do-it-yourself model of the Concorde too. And for the budding technologist, science comes to life with lots of projects and experiments.

The Viking Press   New York

Contents

Information stars

When you come to a star ★ in the story look for another one, in a box, like the one shown here. These know-how boxes explain how things work.

Red boxes

Red boxes point out projects to make and quick experiments to try. There are simple instructions and diagrams to follow for each one. All you will need are a few easy-to-get materials.

Bird's-eye view of an airport

The world of flying is always exciting—even more so when you know what is going on. So first let's take a bird's-eye view of where any air journey begins or ends—the airport.

Airports are all shapes and sizes but they are organized to work in the same way, getting the aircraft up and down safely and moving passengers quickly. Center of operations is the control tower where a team of people directs planes both on the airport and in the sky for miles around. There's a lot more happening behind the scenes too—x-ray machines that see through baggage, microwave-operated doors and baggage conveyors run by photocells.

This is an aerial view of Schiphol airport in Holland. A red line on the diagram shows how the four main runways relate to the part you can see in the photograph. Many airports need more than one runway to cope with different wind conditions.

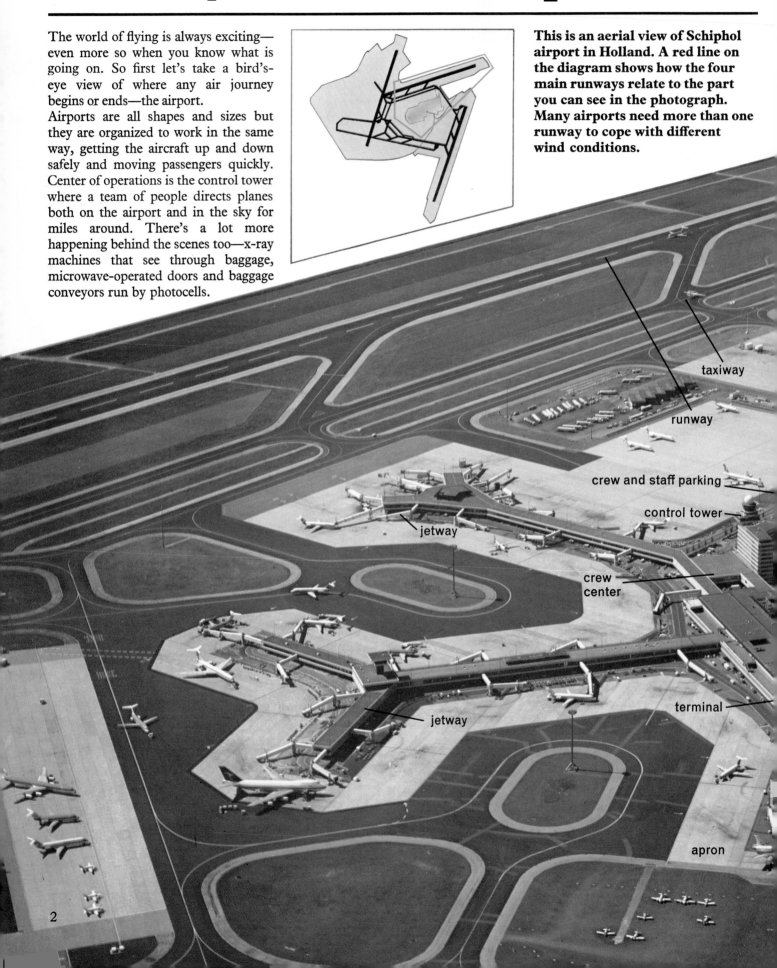

taxiway

runway

crew and staff parking

control tower

jetway

crew center

jetway

terminal

apron

cargo

hotel

Here is the key point of any airport: the control tower. This one is at Orly airport in France.

unfinished underground railroad station

bus station

passenger parking

concourse

Making the reservation

Airlines have reservation offices in every major city. Within minutes an agent can confirm a flight, reserve a seat on the plane and issue a ticket! There's no fuss, no long form to fill in . . . the agent just presses a few buttons. What's the secret?

It's all done by computer

An airline's reservations are stored by computer. All offices are linked to the airline's computer, which may be anywhere. For example, British Airways offices the world over deal with their computer at London's Heathrow Airport, and British Caledonian offices deal with a computer that happens to be in Los Angeles!

A reservation agent uses the VDU in a British Caledonian Airways office to check this family's travel plans.

The Visual Display Unit
Messages sent to the computer and its replies show up on this TV-type screen.
The VDU can find out what flights there are, take bookings, list fares, or send special instructions to the computer about what a passenger wants, such as vegetarian meals. It can even arrange an entire around-the-world trip complete with hotel reservations.

The VDU is linked with the computer by telephone lines, often covering thousands of miles.

These buttons have numbers, letters and symbols for typing information into the computer or 'asking it' questions.

What happens when a customer books a ticket? First, he'll probably ask about available flights on the day he'd like to travel. The agent calls up the computer using the VDU (Visual Display Unit) on the desk. The answer flashes back on the screen within seconds, and the customer chooses a flight. To save time and space an international code ★ based on the English language is used.

To reserve a seat, the agent types into the computer a reservation, the customer's name and where he can be contacted if the flight is changed. Once this information is stored in the computer the reservation is made. The agent issues the ticket in a thin paper folder.

★ Cracking the code

```
1 LHR JFK 15-1800 15-2050  F7YA BA 591 VCX

2 LHR JFK 16-1100 16-1335  F7YA BA 501 747

3 LHR JFK 16-1200 16-1535  F7YA AI 107 747

4 LHR JFK 16-1800 16-2050  F7YA BA 591 VCX

5 LHR JFK 17-1100 17-1335  F7YA BA 501 747
```

Imagine you want to fly from London to New York on March 16. The reservation agent asks the computer about flights and this is how the computer replies on the VDU screen.

Take line 2 as an example. It means 'This flight leaves Heathrow at 11:00 am on March 16, arriving at Kennedy at 13:35 (1:35 pm). You can reserve up to seven first-class seats (F7) and a number of tourist-class seats (Y is the code for tourist or economy class). The flight is BA501 and the plane is a Boeing 747 (a Jumbo jet)'.

See how the code saves space! You decide to take this flight, so the agent types in N1Y2— meaning 'reserve one (N1) tourist-class seat on flight 2 on the list'.

The computer

The computer's brain is the CPU (Central Processor Unit). Its memory keeps track of millions of things at once. This unit 'answers' the VDU.

In here are disks like LPs covered with magnetic recording material. They store airline's reservations, flight details and all the information the CPU needs.

Once a day reservation details are recorded from the disks onto high-speed tape recorders in case of accidents to the disks.

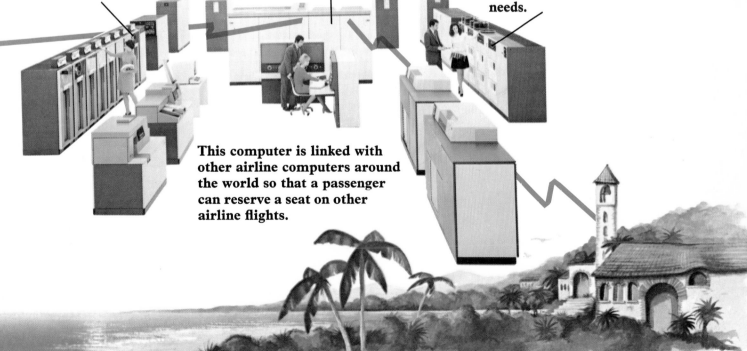

This computer is linked with other airline computers around the world so that a passenger can reserve a seat on other airline flights.

Know your planes

What kind of planes do most people fly in? Plane spotting takes practice but after a while you'll find that you can identify a plane quickly. Points to look for are the number and location of the engines and the shape of the tail or nose. There are different versions of some planes. The 'stretched' DC-8 shown here is longer than the normal one, which looks much like a Boeing 707. To tell the difference, look out for the features shown in the circles—a 707 has a higher nose and a tube at the top of the tail.

Another different version is the 747 SP (special performance) which is shorter than the normal Jumbo but carries fewer passengers over greater range.

**All planes
are drawn to scale
(but not the details)**
L = Length
W = Wingspan

Four engines on wings

Boeing 707 (medium)
L: 44 m (144 ft) W: 40 or 46 m (131 or 151 ft)

Boeing 747 (extra-large)
L: 71 or 54 m (SP) (233 or 177 ft)   W: 60 m (197 ft)

McDonnell Douglas DC-8
(medium-large)
L: 46 or 57 m (151 or 187 ft)
W: 43 or 45 m (141 or 148 ft)

Two engines on wings

Airbus A-300 (large)
L: 54 m (177 ft) W: 45 m (148 ft)

Boeing 737 (small)
L: 30 m (98 ft)
W: 28 m (92 ft)

How far away is that plane?

Here's how to make a simple sighting device to tell you the distance of any plane. You must be able to recognize the plane so you know whether it's a small, medium or large type, and then you can work out its distance from the distance chart. The selection of drawings above will help you classify your plane.

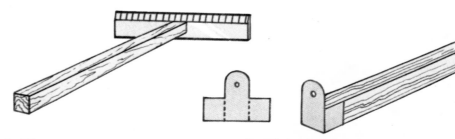

1 The measurer
Tape the ruler to the wood so you can read the millimeter scale when you look from the other end.

2 The sight
Make a tiny hole in a piece of cardboard with a thumbtack. Tape it to the end of the wood.

You will need:
a piece of wood 50 cm (20 in.) long, a 15 cm (6 in.) ruler (transparent, if possible) with millimeter scale, thin cardboard (cereal box will do), tape, thumbtacks, scissors, pencil and paper clips.

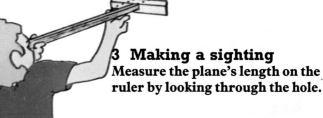

3 Making a sighting
Measure the plane's length on the ruler by looking through the hole.

Two engines on wings, one on tail

Rear-mounted engines

McDonnell Douglas DC-10 (large)
L: 55 m (180 ft) W: 49 m (161 ft)

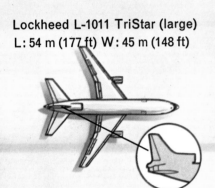

Hawker Siddeley Trident (small)
L: 35 or 40 m (115 or 131 ft)
W: 30 m (98 ft)

McDonnell Douglas DC-9 (small)
L: 38 m (125 ft)
W: 28 m (92 ft)

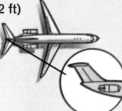

Lockheed L-1011 TriStar (large)
L: 54 m (177 ft) W: 45 m (148 ft)

BAC One-Eleven (small)
L: 29 or 33 m (95 or 108 ft)
W: 29 m (95 ft)

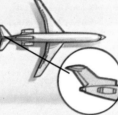

BAC Super VC10 (medium)
L: 52 m (171 ft)
W: 45 m (148 ft)

Boeing 727 (medium)
L: 41 or 47 m (135 or
154 ft) W: 33 m (108 ft)

4 Finding the distance

Decide whether the plane is large, medium or small. Find your measurement of the plane at the bottom of the distance chart. Look straight up the chart until you meet the curve for your size of plane.

Lay a ruler across the chart at this point, parallel with the bottom of the chart. Look across to the left to find how far away the plane is.

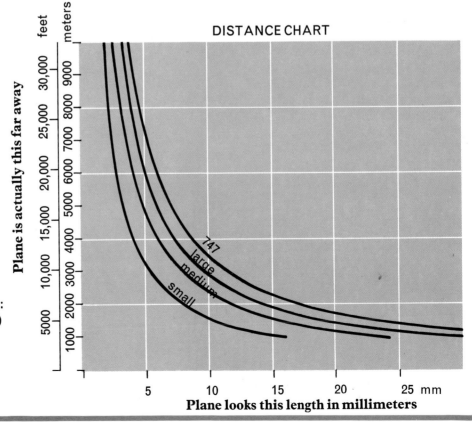

DISTANCE CHART

Plane is actually this far away

feet / meters

747
large
medium
small

Plane looks this length in millimeters

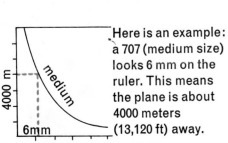

Here is an example: a 707 (medium size) looks 6 mm on the ruler. This means the plane is about 4000 meters (13,120 ft) away.

The day of the flight

At the start of the day, the passengers, the new crew and their plane are all in different places. This page shows how they come together in time for a flight departing at 11:00 am.

The aircraft

Early in the morning on the day of the flight, the plane is hundreds of miles from the airport with a different crew. An hour before they're due to land, this flight crew radios to the airport details of faults that have been found on the aircraft.

At 8:32 am the plane lands, and a few minutes later its passengers get off. Now the maintenance engineers give it a thorough check and begin the work of correcting any faults.

The plane is refueled and fresh provisions are brought on board.

Passengers and crew

Meanwhile, the passengers for the 11:00 flight are checking in and their baggage is being taken to be stored in the hold of the plane. In another part of the airport, the new flight crew gets together.

By departure time, the passengers and the new crew are on the plane, ready to go. On the next few pages, you'll find details of many of the things that are happening on this page.

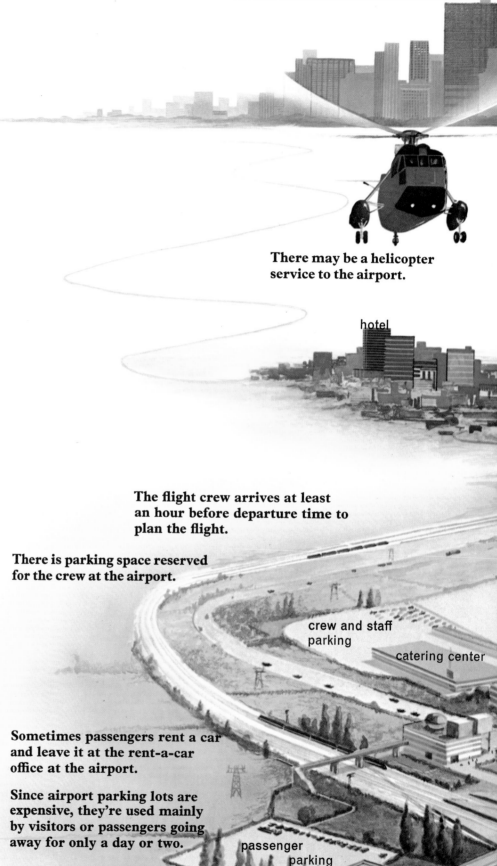

There may be a helicopter service to the airport.

hotel

The flight crew arrives at least an hour before departure time to plan the flight.

There is parking space reserved for the crew at the airport.

crew and staff parking

catering center

Sometimes passengers rent a car and leave it at the rent-a-car office at the airport.

Since airport parking lots are expensive, they're used mainly by visitors or passengers going away for only a day or two.

passenger parking

long-term parking

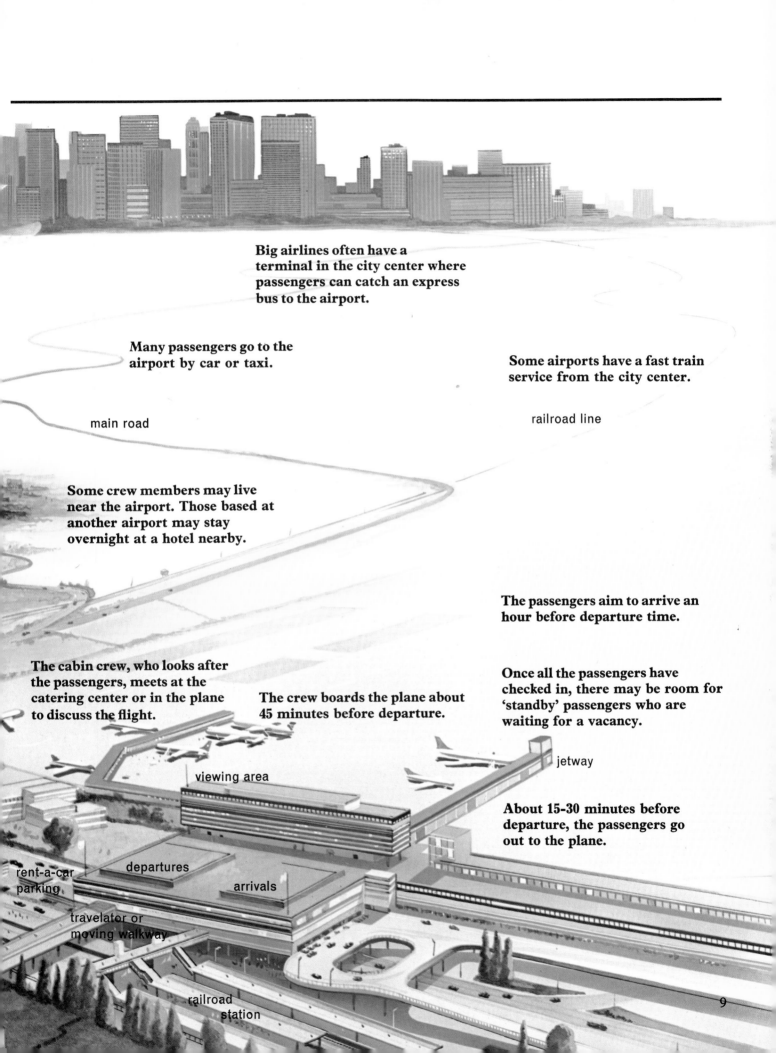

Big airlines often have a terminal in the city center where passengers can catch an express bus to the airport.

Many passengers go to the airport by car or taxi.

Some airports have a fast train service from the city center.

main road

railroad line

Some crew members may live near the airport. Those based at another airport may stay overnight at a hotel nearby.

The passengers aim to arrive an hour before departure time.

The cabin crew, who looks after the passengers, meets at the catering center or in the plane to discuss the flight.

The crew boards the plane about 45 minutes before departure.

Once all the passengers have checked in, there may be room for 'standby' passengers who are waiting for a vacancy.

jetway

viewing area

About 15-30 minutes before departure, the passengers go out to the plane.

rent-a-car parking

departures

arrivals

travelator or moving walkway

railroad station

9

Arriving at the terminal

Most airports have a viewing area where members of the public can watch airplanes and see the layout of the airport, even if they are not going on a journey themselves. There may even be telescopes, and a loudspeaker system to explain what is going on.

International airport terminals are often designed on two levels so that arriving and departing passengers do not get in each other's way.

Inside there are restaurants, stores, bookstores, banks, rest areas and maybe even a movie theater. Friends of departing passengers are allowed into the main hall to see them off.

Passengers arriving at the airport's departure terminal are often loaded with luggage. As if by magic, the doors open automatically ★ for them, and they step inside to find a vast hall with people bound for different places.

★ What makes automatic doors open?

In some cases, a switch under a pressure mat controls the automatic doors. The weight of a person or luggage cart is enough to make the switch operate. (A small child may need to jump on the mat to make it work!)

The most modern system doesn't use a mat. Look above the door and you may see a box: this contains a microwave transmitter and receiver. Microwaves are a type of radio wave, halfway between sound radio and light waves. When the beam of microwaves reflects off an approaching person, the receiver picks up a signal and opens the door.

(These units were developed from a type of burglar alarm which is set off whenever anyone moves about in a room.)

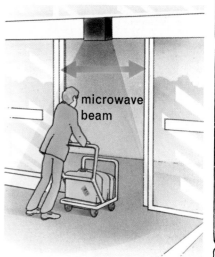

microwave beam

Left: here is a close-up of the main terminal at Schiphol included in the bird's-eye view on pages 2-3. Departing passengers drive up the slope to the second-floor level, while arrivals use the first floor.

See-through moving walkways —called travelators—link various levels of this space-age circular terminal at Charles de Gaulle airport outside Paris. Travelators work just like flat escalators, carrying people about effortlessly.

Below: it's very important to plan airport buildings so that there is plenty of space since each Jumbo can carry about 400 people. If fog or other problems prevent the planes from taking off, all the delayed passengers will still be in the terminal as new ones arrive!

There are two main types of information board giving details of flights, destinations and departure times. One looks like a TV screen. The other kind, shown here, is called a flap indicator board. A light flashes on against the flight number when passengers should start boarding.

Check-in and baggage handling

The departure terminal may well be crowded with hundreds of passengers trying to catch several different flights. Since loading a plane takes time, the passengers usually have to 'check in' their baggage well in advance.

The passengers report to the check-in desk for their flight. Here the check-in operator takes their tickets, asks which seats the passengers would like and hands over the boarding passes.

Off goes the baggage

The baggage is weighed on a platform beside the desk. Usually 20 kg (44 lb) of baggage (30 kg or 66 lb for first class) is allowed. Any extra has to be paid for. The check-in operator fastens labels to the baggage, marked with the destination and flight number.

Then the operator touches a button and the weighing platform—which is in fact a short conveyor—rolls the cases onto the main conveyor behind the check-in desks.

Whenever there is a change of direction or level, the baggage rolls smoothly

QANTAS · BRITISH AIRWAYS · PAN AM · main conveyor · weighing platform · CHECK-IN DESKS · cutaway floor

How photocells work

The photocells which control the conveyors work like electronic switches, operated by beams of light.
As long as a photocell can 'see' the beam, it sends a signal to a computer which allows electric current to operate the main conveyor. But when the beam is blocked by a suitcase, the photocell cuts off the signal. In this way the computer keeps track of suitcases, preventing collisions by stopping sections of the conveyor. (The same sort of photocells are used in some museums and elevators to open doors or count people.)

1. The green and black suitcases are on a collision course.

2. The black one breaks the beam on the carousel. So when the green one breaks its beam, that section of conveyor stops for two seconds.

3. After the two seconds the black one is clear so the green one is allowed to move. But the blue one stops until the green suitcase is clear of the beam.

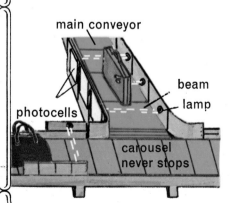

main conveyor · photocells · beam · lamp · carousel never stops

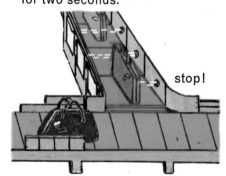

stop!

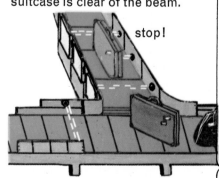

stop! · main conveyor

onto a new section of the main conveyor. Each section is a long loop of canvas or rubber moving around two rollers. (You can make a rubber band run round two pencils in the same way.)

Down to the carousel

The baggage disappears into the handling area where it rolls onto the conveyor. A system of photocells ★ —'magic eyes'—prevents the baggage joining the conveyor from colliding with suitcases already on it. Handlers stand around the carousel, ready to pick up the baggage and load it onto trailers. Suitcases for Jumbos are packed into big containers. This saves time when loading and unloading the plane.

Jumbo container

baggage handlers

carousel

main conveyor

photocells

sections of conveyor

trailer

BAGGAGE HANDLING AREA

Getting the plane ready

A jet aircraft works hard for a living. After a flight the crew members can go home and put their feet up, but the plane must quickly be spruced up and refueled for another flight. The 'turn-around time' for a small jet such as a Trident or Concorde can be under an hour. A big plane such as a Jumbo or TriStar needs about three hours.

The schedule for a Jumbo

8:32 When the plane comes to a halt the ground crew puts blocks under the front wheels and connects an electric power unit. Then the pilot shuts down the jets.

8:35 Mobile steps are put in place for passengers. A freight elevator unloads the baggage.

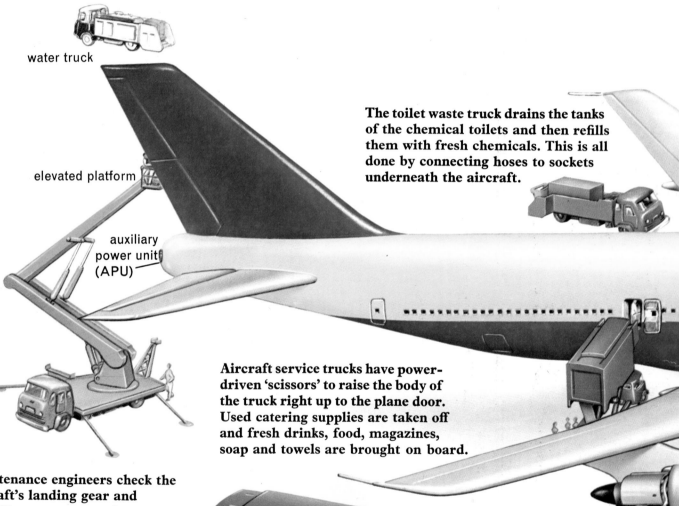

water truck

elevated platform

auxiliary power unit (APU)

The toilet waste truck drains the tanks of the chemical toilets and then refills them with fresh chemicals. This is all done by connecting hoses to sockets underneath the aircraft.

Aircraft service trucks have power-driven 'scissors' to raise the body of the truck right up to the plane door. Used catering supplies are taken off and fresh drinks, food, magazines, soap and towels are brought on board.

Maintenance engineers check the aircraft's landing gear and tires. To carry out on-the-spot repairs they use a mobile platform which can be raised to the top of the plane's tail.

service truck

Blocks stop the plane from moving when the brakes are released for cooling. Brakes get very hot during landing because they slow down the entire weight of the plane. They cool quicker when they are released.

blocks

14

8·44 Various other service trucks roll up, carrying the catering supplies and cleaners' equipment.

8·49 The maintenance engineers begin to check the aircraft systems. They repair any faults.

8·52 Beneath the plane, the toilet waste truck gets to work while another truck fills up the water tanks.

10·00 The refueling begins. The fuel must be balanced evenly among the tanks, three in each wing of a Jumbo. The fuel in the tanks from the previous flight is checked using measuring sticks which pull down from under the wings. A Jumbo's tanks can take up to 175,000 liters (38,500 gallons) of fuel.

10·10 During the time it takes to put the fuel aboard—around 50 minutes for a full load—the captain agrees to the final amount of fuel, which is radioed to the aircraft.

10·15 The flight crew arrives to check the aircraft instruments while the cabin staff sees that all the emergency apparatus is in place.

Air conditioning trucks may pump fresh air of a comfortable temperature into the aircraft.

The mobile steps have 'feet' which are lowered to keep them firmly in place. (Steps are only used when the plane is not using a jetway.)

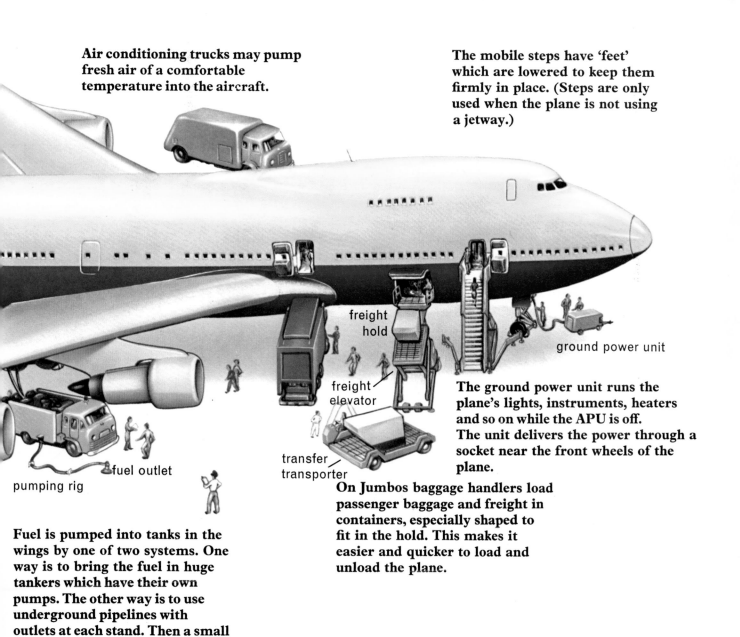

freight hold

ground power unit

freight elevator

transfer transporter

fuel outlet

pumping rig

The ground power unit runs the plane's lights, instruments, heaters and so on while the APU is off. The unit delivers the power through a socket near the front wheels of the plane.

On Jumbos baggage handlers load passenger baggage and freight in containers, especially shaped to fit in the hold. This makes it easier and quicker to load and unload the plane.

Fuel is pumped into tanks in the wings by one of two systems. One way is to bring the fuel in huge tankers which have their own pumps. The other way is to use underground pipelines with outlets at each stand. Then a small rig pumps in the fuel.

The flight crew prepares

'*Reports of CAT★ here . . . better flight at 39,000 feet . . .*'

'*We've 324 passengers today. One of the runways at our destination is closed . . . we may have to go on and use the alternate airport.*'

To the flight crew—the captain, first officer and flight engineer—this discussion is just part of another day's work, but it happens long before the plane is in the air. An hour or so before departure, the crew reports to flight dispatch, where the important job of preflight planning begins.

All the news . . .

Are all radio beacons along the route in working order? Is the destination airport open? Any military testing sites being used today? The crew receives latest news of possible hazards and problems before takeoff. The captain starts by discussing latest reports on the condition of the aircraft. It is up to him whether or not to accept that

The crew discusses the flight plan. Once this has been agreed on, the captain signs it and files it with air traffic control.

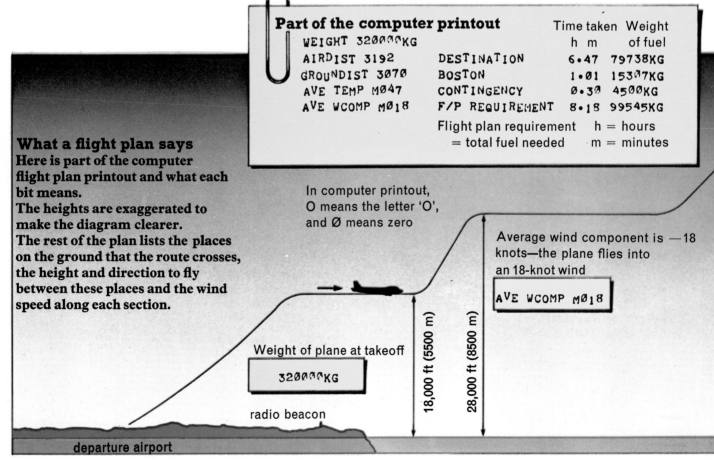

Part of the computer printout

WEIGHT 32000KG
AIRDIST 3192
GROUNDIST 3070
AVE TEMP M047
AVE WCOMP M018

	Time taken h m	Weight of fuel
DESTINATION	6•47	79738KG
BOSTON	1•01	15307KG
CONTINGENCY	0•30	4500KG
F/P REQUIREMENT	8•18	99545KG

Flight plan requirement = total fuel needed

h = hours   m = minutes

What a flight plan says
Here is part of the computer flight plan printout and what each bit means.
The heights are exaggerated to make the diagram clearer.
The rest of the plan lists the places on the ground that the route crosses, the height and direction to fly between these places and the wind speed along each section.

In computer printout, O means the letter 'O', and Ø means zero

Average wind component is —18 knots—the plane flies into an 18-knot wind

AVE WCOMP M018

Weight of plane at takeoff

32000KG

radio beacon

18,000 ft (5500 m)

28,000 ft (8500 m)

departure airport

plane. If the faults are minor he will probably give it the OK.

What's the weather like?
Since the weather plays a large part in deciding the flight plan, the crew must look at the latest weather maps and may also study photos of cloud cover radioed directly to the airport from satellites in space.

This information helps to choose the best route. The crew will know what to expect along the way.

How much fuel?
A few hours before the flight, airline staff members work out the best possible routes. The flight crew studies these in the light of the latest weather and hazard information. Where there is a choice of safe routes, the crew usually picks the one which needs least fuel.

The final fuel figure is then radioed to the plane so that the tanks can be filled up to the right level.

Beware of the CAT

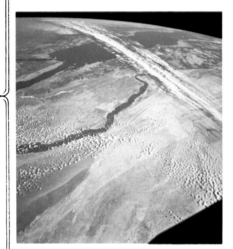

Satellite view of a jet stream

Certain types of weather are enemies of planes—and the worst are thunderclouds and CAT (Clear Air Turbulence). Pilots try to avoid these since sudden upward currents make the air bumpy. In the case of CAT, there aren't even any warning clouds, but it is usually found near jet streams—high-speed rivers of air flowing at up to 320 km/h (198.4 mph) at a height of about 30,000 ft (10,000 meters).

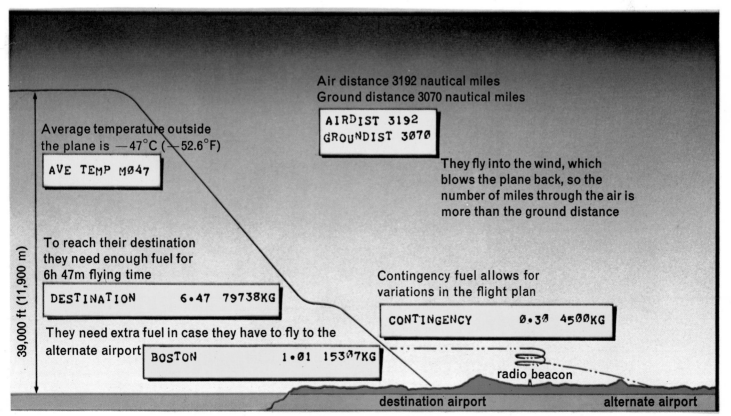

Air distance 3192 nautical miles
Ground distance 3070 nautical miles

AIRDIST 3192
GROUNDIST 3070

They fly into the wind, which blows the plane back, so the number of miles through the air is more than the ground distance

Average temperature outside the plane is —47°C (—52.6°F)

AVE TEMP M047

To reach their destination they need enough fuel for 6h 47m flying time

DESTINATION   6•47 79738KG

Contingency fuel allows for variations in the flight plan

CONTINGENCY   0•30 4500KG

They need extra fuel in case they have to fly to the alternate airport

BOSTON   1•01 15307KG

39,000 ft (11,900 m)

radio beacon

destination airport

alternate airport

What's where on a Jumbo

A Jumbo can carry up to 500 passengers, though a more usual load is about 300. The passengers sit up to ten across. Because of its width, a Jumbo is called a 'wide-bodied' jet. It has two aisles.

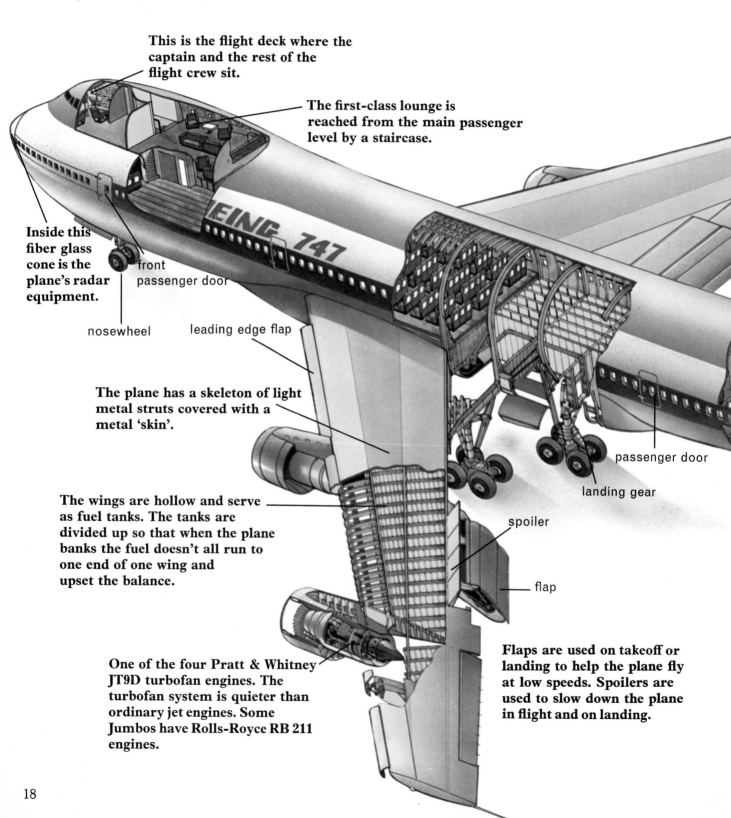

This is the flight deck where the captain and the rest of the flight crew sit.

The first-class lounge is reached from the main passenger level by a staircase.

Inside this fiber glass cone is the plane's radar equipment.

front passenger door

nosewheel

leading edge flap

The plane has a skeleton of light metal struts covered with a metal 'skin'.

The wings are hollow and serve as fuel tanks. The tanks are divided up so that when the plane banks the fuel doesn't all run to one end of one wing and upset the balance.

One of the four Pratt & Whitney JT9D turbofan engines. The turbofan system is quieter than ordinary jet engines. Some Jumbos have Rolls-Royce RB 211 engines.

passenger door

landing gear

spoiler

flap

Flaps are used on takeoff or landing to help the plane fly at low speeds. Spoilers are used to slow down the plane in flight and on landing.

18

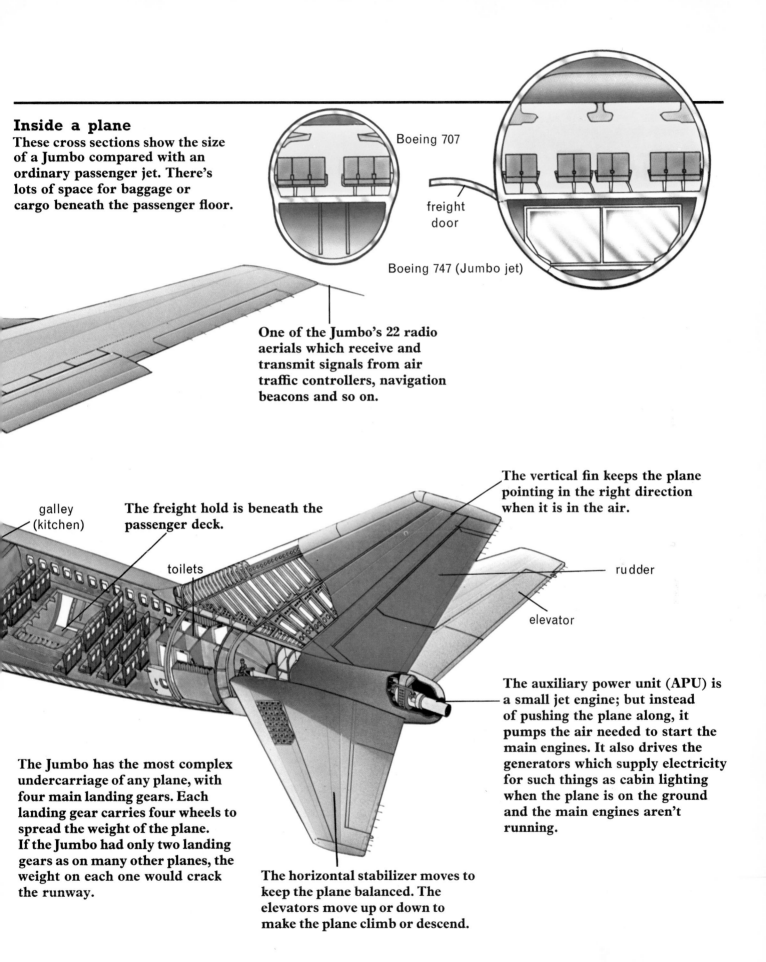

Inside a plane

These cross sections show the size of a Jumbo compared with an ordinary passenger jet. There's lots of space for baggage or cargo beneath the passenger floor.

Boeing 707

freight door

Boeing 747 (Jumbo jet)

One of the Jumbo's 22 radio aerials which receive and transmit signals from air traffic controllers, navigation beacons and so on.

galley (kitchen)

The freight hold is beneath the passenger deck.

toilets

The vertical fin keeps the plane pointing in the right direction when it is in the air.

rudder

elevator

The Jumbo has the most complex undercarriage of any plane, with four main landing gears. Each landing gear carries four wheels to spread the weight of the plane. If the Jumbo had only two landing gears as on many other planes, the weight on each one would crack the runway.

The auxiliary power unit (APU) is a small jet engine; but instead of pushing the plane along, it pumps the air needed to start the main engines. It also drives the generators which supply electricity for such things as cabin lighting when the plane is on the ground and the main engines aren't running.

The horizontal stabilizer moves to keep the plane balanced. The elevators move up or down to make the plane climb or descend.

`Please proceed to Gate 6...'

At every airport, there are certain points beyond which only passengers may go—visitors are not allowed. So the passengers say good-bye to their friends and go to the departure lounge.

Security checks

On the way they show their boarding passes to a controller to prove that they're genuine passengers. International flight passengers must also let the passport officer look at their passports.

Airlines have to prevent the wrong people, especially hijackers, getting aboard the planes. Someone managing to smuggle a gun or a bomb on board could cause a fatal disaster. To stop this, passengers are checked with a metal detector for illegal metal objects they might have hidden on themselves. As well as searching passengers, security also x-rays hand baggage for any suspicious objects.

Getting to the plane

Having cleared security, passengers sit around in the departure lounge and wait to hear that their plane is ready for boarding:

'Will passengers please proceed to Gate 6...'
They may walk straight onto the plane along an extending jetway or go by bus if their waiting plane is a long way from the terminal.

On the plane

At last the passengers step aboard the plane. After the bustle of the airport, it is a different world—everything seems hushed and soft music plays to soothe the anxious. Passengers find their seats by number and begin to investigate their surroundings.

X-raying luggage
Baggage inspectors may put hand baggage into a special x-ray machine.
X-rays are invisible, but they can pass right through most things. Only metal blocks x-rays well.
Inside the x-ray machine is a special plate which turns x-rays into light. A TV camera views this plate, and can zoom in on any part of it. What the camera sees is displayed on the screen. A suitcase in the x-ray beam looks transparent on the screen, but any metal objects inside it show up black!

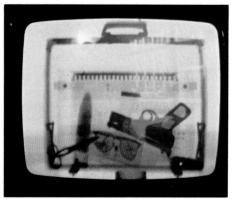

As soon as the hatch closes something happens secretly. Inside the compartment is a 'sniffer'—it samples the air circulating round the case for traces of the smell of explosives. Even if there's only a lingering smell of explosives on a pair of gloves, the 'sniffer' can still pick it out and ring an alarm.

Searching people
This metal detector has coils on both sides of an archway. The passenger walks through while a guard watches a needle on a dial which shows the amount of metal present. (These machines do not use x-rays.)

Passengers use mobile steps to climb into the plane if they go out by bus.

Here is the huge tourist section of the Jumbo. There are two aisles so passengers can walk around and stretch their legs.

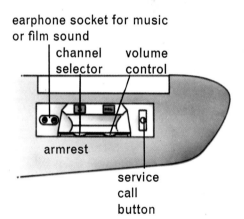

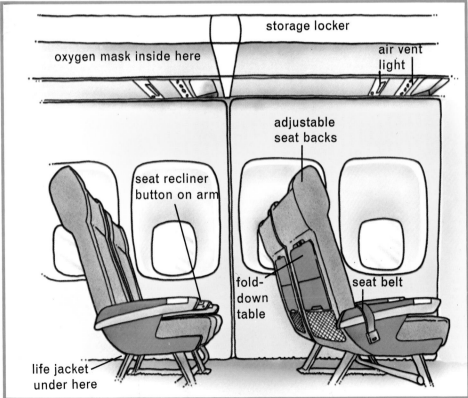

storage locker

oxygen mask inside here

air vent
light

adjustable
seat backs

seat recliner
button on arm

fold-
down
table

seat belt

life jacket
under here

earphone socket for music
or film sound

channel
selector

volume
control

armrest

service
call
button

Safety first

During takeoff and landing, passengers must wear seat belts and keep their seat backs upright to stop them from being thrown around in an emergency. Since the plane will be flying at high altitudes, oxygen masks are carried in case the air pressure system inside the plane fails.

Safety first: pre-flight checks

As the passengers are being searched, the flight crew begins the preflight checks of the aircraft. The crew can't take chances that something might not be working.

The flight engineer walks slowly round the outside of the plane to ensure that nothing is obviously wrong. When he is satisfied, he joins the pilot and first officer on the flight deck. Here the crew checks all the plane's instruments, systems and controls.

All set for the flight

Some instruments must be fed with information. The altimeters, which tell the plane's height, are set to read either zero or the height of the airport above sea level. Clocks need setting to a radio time signal. The captain sets the navigation system to the plane's exact position to give it a starting point.

The crew tests each instrument in turn, checking its reading. Some systems, such as the hydraulics which work the brakes and undercarriage, can only be checked when the engines are running.

Starting up

Big jet engines are too large to be started by an electric motor, so there's a smaller jet engine at the back of the plane, the Auxiliary Power Unit (APU), which does the job. It produces compressed air to start the turbines in the main jet engines. The APU also runs a generator for the plane's electric power.

The flight engineer checks the plane. Have all the maintenance panels underneath been properly closed? Are the tires OK? Are any of the fuel or oil pipes leaking? Do the blades of the jet turbines look all right?

Key to the color code

Aircraft systems

Flying instruments

Engine instruments

Flying controls

Communications panel

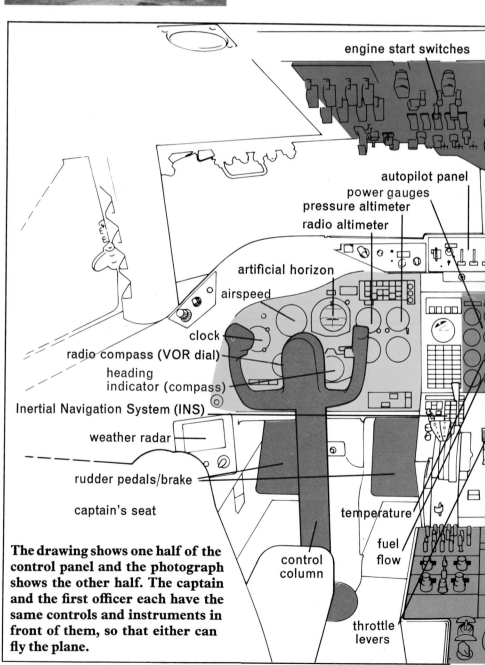

engine start switches

autopilot panel
power gauges
pressure altimeter
radio altimeter

artificial horizon

airspeed

clock

radio compass (VOR dial)

heading indicator (compass)

Inertial Navigation System (INS)

weather radar

rudder pedals/brake

captain's seat

control column

temperature

fuel flow

throttle levers

The drawing shows one half of the control panel and the photograph shows the other half. The captain and the first officer each have the same controls and instruments in front of them, so that either can fly the plane.

22

Who's who

Big jets need only three people
to fly them. In charge is the
captain who always sits in the left-
hand seat.
The first officer or copilot
sits on the right; and behind them,
facing sideways, is the flight
engineer. (The word *pilot* is used
for whoever is flying the plane.)
In the photograph, the engineer
is taking readings from instruments
and entering them in the logbook.

Starting the engines

All crew members help to start
the main engines one at a time.
●The flight engineer flicks a
switch and the APU starts
turning the engine.
●The first officer times each
stage because if the engines
don't start within a certain
time something is wrong.
●The captain watches the engine
speed build up on a dial in front
of him and, at the right speed,
switches on the fuel flow and
the engine roars into life.

Most flight instruments have
little red warning 'flags' or
lights which appear if anything is
wrong or the instrument isn't
switched on.
Others have 'push to test'
buttons on them to check that
they work.

Taxiing out

The engines have been started and everyone is ready to go! But the captain can't move off (called taxiing) until the control tower gives permission.

One air traffic controller looks after all the aircraft on the ground and no plane can move without his permission. When visibility is poor, the controller can see exactly where the planes are on a radar ★ screen. It gives an instant view of the whole airport, whatever the weather.

The captain tells the controller he is ready to leave, and soon clearance comes from the control tower:
'*Speedbird 501, to runway two eight left*'.

Runway names

Runways are named according to the direction in which they point, using the 360 degrees of the magnetic compass. So runway 'two eight' points towards 280°, which is just to the north of west. Where there are two parallel runways, they are called right and left.

The plane begins its slow journey to the beginning of the runway, using the jet engines at low power. Unlike a car, the wheels of a plane are not driven—the plane just rolls along on them.

At busy airports, there is often a line of planes waiting to take off at what is called the holding point. The captain joins the line and radios the control tower for further instructions.

Inside the control tower
The plane and the control tower are linked by radio. All conversations between planes on the ground and their controller happen on a single channel so that planes can listen to one another. Every plane has a call sign, usually the same as its flight number on the timetable.

Planes can't go into reverse—so moving backward to clear the airport buildings is a problem.
An aircraft tug must push a plane backward by the nosewheel.
One little tug is powerful enough to push a 385-ton fully loaded Jumbo.
While the plane is still on the ground, the captain can steer it using a small handle beside him, which turns the nosewheel to left or right.

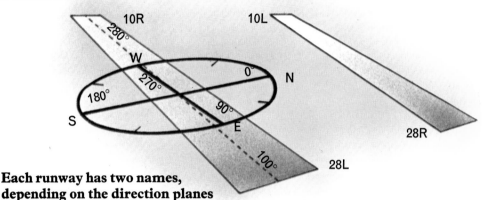
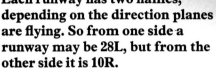

Each runway has two names, depending on the direction planes are flying. So from one side a runway may be 28L, but from the other side it is 10R.

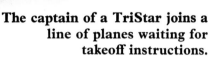

The captain of a TriStar joins a line of planes waiting for takeoff instructions.

How radar works

Radar is a way of giving a radio picture of an area. Since radio waves are not stopped by fog (you can pick up radio programs just as well when it's foggy as when it's clear), they give a picture even in poor visibility. You normally see things because light shines on them. To 'see' things by radar, you need a radio transmitter to send out beams of radio waves. This is done by a scanner which takes only a few seconds to make a full sweep. Its beams bounce off the things around and return, like echoes. Radio waves travel fast— nearly 300,000 km (186,000 mi) a second!

So the journey to and from an object 1 km (.62 mi) away takes under 70 millionths of a second. As the echoes return, they are shown on a circular screen. This has a glowing trace which sweeps around at the same rate as the scanner.

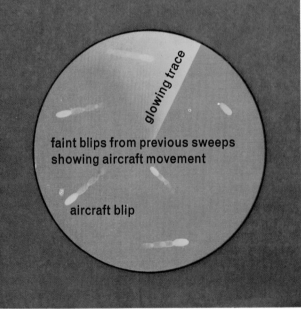

glowing trace

faint blips from previous sweeps showing aircraft movement

aircraft blip

On the screen is a radio map of the area with objects showing as 'blips'. These stay glowing after the trace has gone by. Every sweep of the trace renews the whole picture.

Ready for take-off

'*Speedbird 501, you are cleared for takeoff.*'

This is the moment everyone has waited for. The giant plane lumbers slowly to the beginning of the runway and lines up with the white line painted down the middle. Over 3 km (1.9 mi) of concrete 90 m (295.2 ft) wide stretch ahead.

An aircraft needs to travel quite fast—about 150 knots (278 km/h) in this case—before it can take off. The crew has already worked out the takeoff speed, which depends on such things as the weather and the weight of the plane at takeoff.

Racing down the runway

To take off, the engines are set to high power so that the plane races down the runway. The crew watches the speed and at the right moment the captain pulls back on the control column to 'rotate' the plane—that is, he brings the nose up so it climbs into the sky. ★

Taking off is always thrilling. The sound of the jets increases to a scream and the whole plane vibrates, pressing its passengers back into their seats as it surges forward. After half a minute or so the plane starts to climb and seconds later there's a muffled thud as the undercarriage lifts.

The flight has begun!

a TriStar moving slowly along a taxiway

Getting up speed

With permission to take off, the captain pushes the throttle levers forward and the engines roar. The crew watches the instruments carefully to check that nothing is wrong.

The copilot calls out the airspeed indicator reading. The first of three important speeds worked out beforehand is V_1, called V-one (V stands for velocity or speed). Above this speed the plane can't stop on the remaining runway—it has to take off.

A few seconds later the plane reaches V_R, the rotation velocity. The captain begins to 'rotate' the plane to point skyward by pulling back on the control column, and the nosewheel lifts off the ground.

typical takeoff speeds and runway distances for a Jumbo	122 knots 940 m (3084 ft)	138 knots 1280 m (41200 ft)
	V_1	V_R

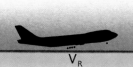

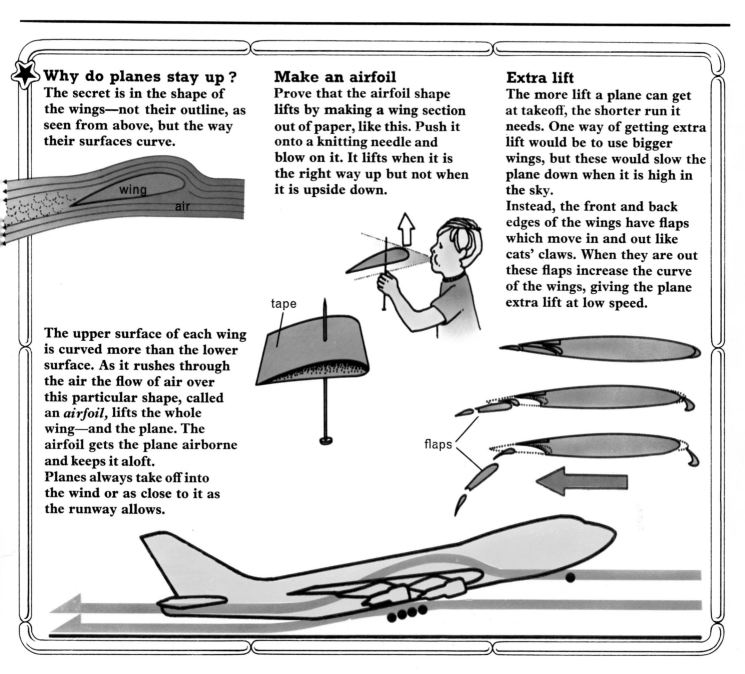

Why do planes stay up?

The secret is in the shape of the wings—not their outline, as seen from above, but the way their surfaces curve.

wing

air

The upper surface of each wing is curved more than the lower surface. As it rushes through the air the flow of air over this particular shape, called an *airfoil*, lifts the whole wing—and the plane. The airfoil gets the plane airborne and keeps it aloft.

Planes always take off into the wind or as close to it as the runway allows.

Make an airfoil

Prove that the airfoil shape lifts by making a wing section out of paper, like this. Push it onto a knitting needle and blow on it. It lifts when it is the right way up but not when it is upside down.

tape

Extra lift

The more lift a plane can get at takeoff, the shorter run it needs. One way of getting extra lift would be to use bigger wings, but these would slow the plane down when it is high in the sky.

Instead, the front and back edges of the wings have flaps which move in and out like cats' claws. When they are out these flaps increase the curve of the wings, giving the plane extra lift at low speed.

flaps

The captain continues to raise the plane's nose. He judges it carefully so that as the copilot calls out V_2 (the climbing speed) the main wheels have just left the ground and the plane is airborne.

148 knots
1,580 m
(5184 ft)

V_2

A-300 Airbus taking off

Up and away

Just imagine. A Jumbo may weigh as much as 406 tons including its fuel, passengers, baggage and cargo. The body of the plane is 71 m (232.9 ft) long from nose to tail and the wing span is 60 m (196.8 ft). And it may stay up for over 4000 miles (about 6400 km) at a time.

To get a jet up in the air you need two things: lift (see pages 26-27) and pushing power, called thrust★. Four great jet engines provide the thrust that drives the plane fast enough to create lift and also keep it moving forward through the air.

A jet engine alone produces a very fierce and noisy gas stream. In a turbofan engine, however, the gas stream drives a large fan which creates a slower blast of air.
This has as much thrust as a simple jet and drives the plane as quickly, but it is quieter.

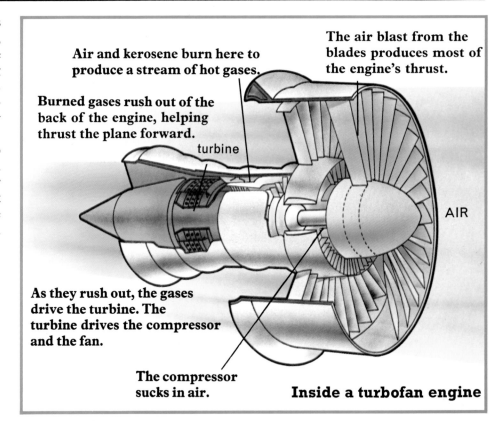

Air and kerosene burn here to produce a stream of hot gases.

The air blast from the blades produces most of the engine's thrust.

Burned gases rush out of the back of the engine, helping thrust the plane forward.

turbine

AIR

As they rush out, the gases drive the turbine. The turbine drives the compressor and the fan.

The compressor sucks in air.

Inside a turbofan engine

What is thrust ?

Think of stepping forward off a skateboard. As you go forward you will find that the skateboard rolls backward.

Or have you ever held a garden hose and asked someone to turn it full on? Suddenly a whoosh of water bursts out and the hose almost jumps out of your hand. As the hose goes one way, you go the other way—and firemen are sometimes pushed over by this backward force.

These are just two examples of one of the basic laws of nature:

'For every force in one direction there is always an equal force in the opposite direction.'

The hot gases in the jet engine expand and rush out of the back of the engine at great speed, in the same way as the water bursts out of the hose. Many people believe that the gases 'push' against the air to propel the plane forward, but this is not true. As the gases shoot out backward so the jet goes forward, obeying that law of nature.

How planes fly

Once in the air, a plane must be steered to keep it flying on course. The pilot steers a plane by tilting it up, down or sideways, or by pointing it to the right or left. To make it do these things control surfaces ★ are used. These are on the edges of the wings and tail and are called elevators, rudder and ailerons.

The control surfaces work by using the rush of air past the plane. Normally they lie flat; but when they are moved they 'bend' the flow of air past them. The airflow pushes the whole surface in one direction in the same way as the airfoil shape of a wing gives it an upward push.

How control surfaces move the plane

Climbing
To take the plane up . . .
- The pilot pulls the control column back
- This moves the elevators up
- Airflow across elevators forces tail down and nose up
- Plane climbs

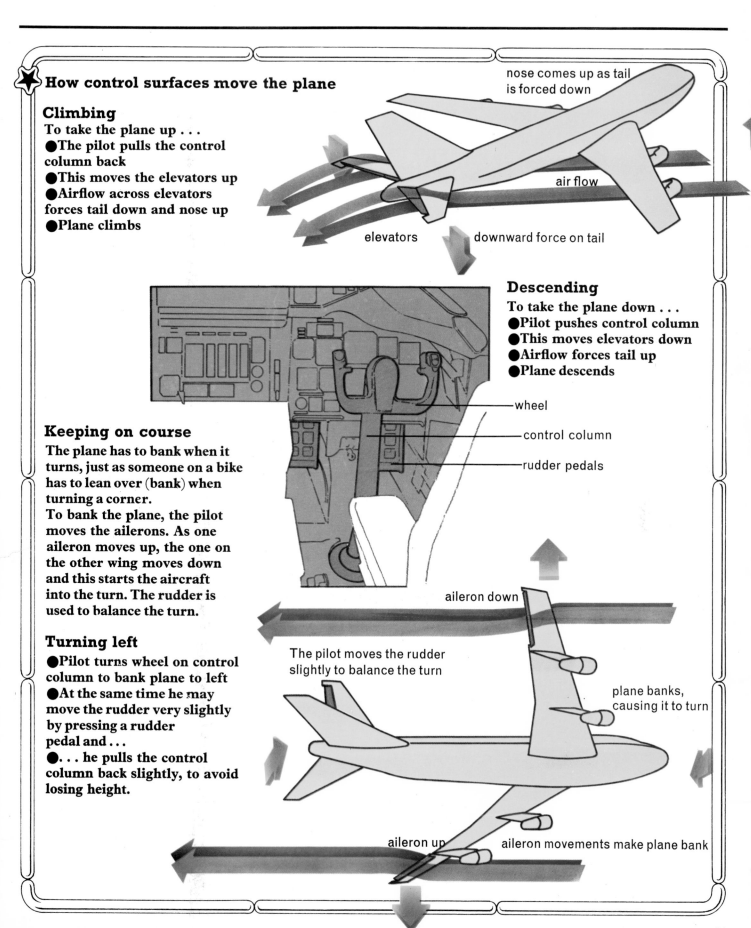

nose comes up as tail is forced down

air flow

elevators

downward force on tail

Descending
To take the plane down . . .
- Pilot pushes control column
- This moves elevators down
- Airflow forces tail up
- Plane descends

wheel

control column

rudder pedals

Keeping on course
The plane has to bank when it turns, just as someone on a bike has to lean over (bank) when turning a corner.
To bank the plane, the pilot moves the ailerons. As one aileron moves up, the one on the other wing moves down and this starts the aircraft into the turn. The rudder is used to balance the turn.

Turning left
- Pilot turns wheel on control column to bank plane to left
- At the same time he may move the rudder very slightly by pressing a rudder pedal and . . .
- . . . he pulls the control column back slightly, to avoid losing height.

aileron down

The pilot moves the rudder slightly to balance the turn

plane banks, causing it to turn

aileron up

aileron movements make plane bank

On the flight deck

Throughout the flight either the captain or the first officer must stay in his seat, watching the plane's flight instruments. The routine work of flying the plane, however, is done by the automatic pilot (autopilot) which keeps the plane level and heading in the right direction.

The pilot's instruments

The pilot relies on instruments when he flies the plane or wants to check that the autopilot is doing its job. The instruments shown on these two pages tell him if the plane is flying level, how high it is and how fast it is traveling. On a Jumbo jet the instruments are more complicated than the ones shown here, but they work in the same way.

Pressure altimeter

A metal capsule inside the altimeter behaves like a balloon. As the air pressure ★ gets less when the plane goes higher, the capsule expands because of the air sealed inside it. This movement drives the altimeter's pointer around.

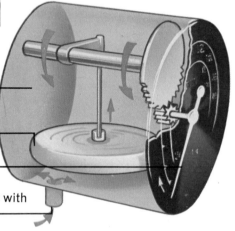

inside of altimeter is sealed off from cabin air

metal capsule with air sealed inside

needle moves to show height

pipe connects altimeter with the outside air

Artificial horizon

This tells the pilot whether the plane is level or not. It uses a gyroscope, a wheel which is kept spinning at high speed. If you have a toy gyroscope, you'll know that it is difficult to tilt it once the wheel is spinning. In the same way, a toy top always stays upright until it starts to slow down. As the plane banks or climbs, the artificial horizon shows what is happening.

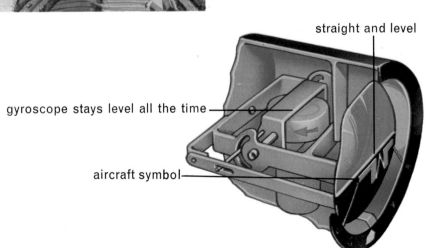

straight and level

gyroscope stays level all the time

aircraft symbol

banking to right

Airspeed indicator

The airspeed indicator also works by air pressure. The force of the air on the front of the plane creates more pressure than there is at the side of the plane. The indicator shows the difference between the two pressures. The faster the plane goes, the greater the difference. To measure this difference, the plane has a *pitot* (pronounced pee-toe) tube sticking out forward into the air stream.

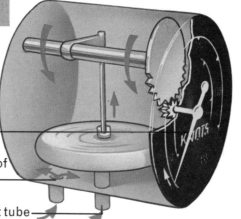

needle shows difference between two pressures, giving airspeed—

air pressure pipe from side of plane—

capsule connected to pitot tube—

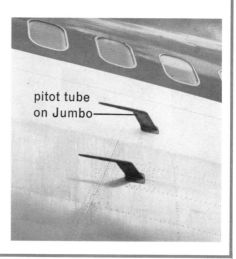

pitot tube on Jumbo—

Air pressure

Air has weight. But you don't feel the air pressing on you because it presses equally in all directions and your body is used to it.

To prove that air has weight, spread an open newspaper over two thirds of a ruler projecting from the edge of a table. Hit the end of the ruler as hard as you like. The weight of air on top of the newspaper keeps it in place. This weight is called pressure.

The higher you go above the Earth's surface, the less air there is above you, so the lower the air pressure is. This means that air pressure is a good guide to height, and an altimeter is a type of pressure gauge.

A balloon filled with air gets bigger as it goes higher because the air pressure inside and out has to be equal. The less the outside pressure tries to push the balloon in, the more the air inside can push it out.

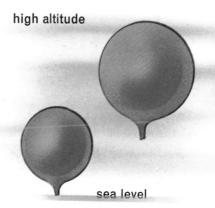

high altitude

sea level

Finding the way

How does a plane find its way?
Pilots of small planes can fly from one landmark to another or follow roads and rivers as long as the ground is visible. But airliner crews need better guidance as their planes are often above unbroken clouds for most of the flight.

The crews of early airliners followed routes by using a compass. But compass readings don't allow for winds blowing the plane off course. Every so often the navigator had to measure the position of the sun or a star with a sextant to get an accurate reading to work from.

Nowadays modern airliners also have complicated electronic systems, such as VOR and DME which use radio signals and INS (see page 36) which uses gyroscopes, to help the pilots and their planes find the way across the sky.

A map called SID

Immediately after takeoff, the captain follows a 'Standard Instrument Depar-ture' or SID—a map of air routes between radio beacons.

An air traffic controller keeps an eye on the plane's progress on a radar screen. When the plane is clear of the airport the controller, who has a copy of the agreed flight plan, radios new instructions to the captain. These instructions tell the captain how to take the plane off the standard instrument departure route and onto the agreed flight plan (explained on pages 16 and 17).

Following SID

After takeoff the SID directs the pilot 'straight ahead to intercept 159R to Lookout VOR. Cross Lookout VOR above 3000 feet'. This means that the pilot is to fly to the 159 radial (line) coming from the Lookout VOR radio beacon. The pilot should then follow this line to the beacon, climbing to cross it above 3000 ft (914 meters).

The VOR dial and its needle each turn separately. The dial shows the direction the plane is heading, while the needle shows the beacon's direction.

VOR radio waves

159° radial

VOR beacon

dial reading 280°
needle reading 339°

airport

Remember: there are 360 degrees in a circle so half a circle has 180°. The 159° radial seen from the plane becomes 339° (159° + 180°).

Tuning to VOR

The captain tunes to the Lookout VOR beacon channel. The VOR dial on the instrument panel looks like a compass but, instead of pointing north, its needle shows the direction of the beacon it is tuned to. After takeoff the pilot turns the plane on to the 159 line. VOR stands for 'VHF Omnidirectional Range' because it broadcasts VHF (Very High Frequency) radio signals in all directions. The crew can find the beacon by following any of the 360 VOR radials. On picking up a signal, the plane's instruments show the direction of the beacon.

In this combined VOR and DME beacon the outer ring is the VOR and the pole in the center is the DME.

The air traffic controllers keep in touch with the crew by radio. As the plane passes from one ATC area to the next, its radio is retuned to different channels.

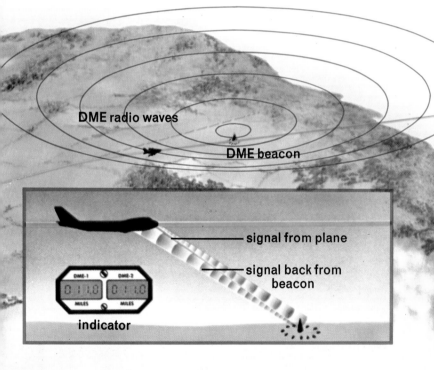

DME radio waves

DME beacon

signal from plane

signal back from beacon

DME-1 DME-2

MILES MILES

indicator

VOR and DME beacons act like signposts, showing the roads in the sky. On short journeys planes follow VORs and DMEs. For long distances they also use the Inertial Navigation System (INS).

DME beacons

The captain flies from one beacon to another as shown on his SID instructions. Then the SID indicates to the captain that 'at 11 DME NTN left turn'. This means to turn left 11 nautical miles (20 km) from the Newton DME beacon. An indicator shows how far it is to the DME beacon.

A transmitter on the plane sends a radio signal to the DME (Distance Measuring Equipment) beacon it's tuned to. When the beacon picks up a signal, it sends back one of its own within millionths of a second. The further the plane is from the beacon, the longer it takes before its receivers pick up the reply.

Over oceans and deserts

Most long-distance planes have an Inertial Navigation System★—INS for short. This complex device keeps track of the plane's location without needing any radio beacons or ground landmarks. Each time the plane changes speed or turns, delicate instruments inside the INS sense what happens, even when the plane flies over oceans and deserts.

Imagine your eyes are closed. You are in a car or bus trying to work out where it's going. From the starting point, you have to try to feel every movement. As the vehicle speeds up, you have to calculate how fast it is going and how far you've gone. Could you be sure where you are after, say, ten minutes? An INS is so sensitive that it can say where a plane is even after five hours of flight.

The INS also relays the direction of the flight to the autopilot. So, when the plane needs to follow a course for a long distance, the crew can switch on the autopilot and let it take over. Since the autopilot is linked to all the flying controls, it can fly the plane by itself.

over the Atlantic all planes within an air corridor must fly at the same speed

air corridor at 33,000 ft (10,058 m)

air corridor at 31,000 ft (9450 m)

★ Inertia points the way
See how inertial navigation works by filling a jug with water and floating a small paper arrow in the middle. Turn the jug slowly. You should find that the paper arrow always points in the same direction.
This is because of the *inertia* of the water it floats on. Inertia means reluctance to move.

If it weren't for the fact that the water soon becomes disturbed when the jug is moved about you could use a device like this to keep pointing in whatever direction you wanted, no matter how much your path turned.

Inside an INS
Planes need a very accurate system of navigation which will measure movements in all directions.
At the heart of an INS unit there is a small platform kept level by gyroscopes, like the artificial horizon on page 32.
On this platform, three accelerometers measure movements.

These accelerometers are at right angles to each other so that they can measure movement in any direction.

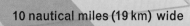

10 nautical miles (19 km) wide

air corridor at 32,000 ft (9754 m)

INS control panel

The INS is really a minicomputer. As well as storing details of the flight plan, it also calculates all sorts of details that the crew might need.

The crew can store up to nine route changes in the memory of the INS. When it completes one section of the flight, the INS automatically changes course on to the next section, giving the autopilot its instructions.

Corridors in the air

To prevent midair collisions, planes fly along air 'corridors'. The aim is to space out all the planes going in one direction and flying at the same height and speed. Since some planes fly slower and lower than others, the air corridors are organized into speed zones. But instead of being side by side, like highway lanes, these zones are in layers above one another.

Autopilot panel

The autopilot can do anything a human pilot can—as long as it is given instructions. The pilot either sets the flight direction himself, or he switches the autopilot to take instructions straight from the INS.

Keeping the customers satisfied

To the passengers, life above the clouds is easy. There's little to do for several hours, and everything seems to be going smoothly.

Yet outside, that world of blue skies, warm sun and white fleecy clouds is hostile. The temperature is far below freezing, and the air pressure is so low that it's too thin to breathe. If a door opened accidentally, the rush of air would suck out anything nearby, and the sudden lack of air would make everyone faint within seconds.

To keep everyone warm and comfortable, the inside of the plane is pressurized★. That means the air pressure is increased so that the air becomes breathable. Even at a high altitude, there is plenty of oxygen in the air. But the air is so spread out that a person would have to breathe about five times more deeply to get the same amount of oxygen into the lungs as on the ground.

Is everybody happy?

Each airline works hard to make its passengers as comfortable as possible, in the hope that they will fly with that airline again. Food is served from the plane's galley (kitchen). This meal service is included in the price of the ticket.

To stop the passengers from getting bored on long flights, there are usually inflight movies and several channels of music to suit all tastes. If you want to listen to the music there is an extra charge for the use of the earphones. You need these to hear the film soundtrack too—but they can't stop those who haven't got the earphones from just looking at the film!

★ **Pressurization**
The pressurized air for a Jumbo's cabin comes from compressors driven by the engines. The compressor sucks in low pressure air from outside, compresses (squeezes) it to make it into higher pressure air, and sends it to the heater. Here it is warmed to a comfortable temperature before being passed to the cabin through vents. Stale air leaves the plane through valves which let the right amount out. This way, all the air in the plane is changed every 90 seconds.

Air pressure is usually measured in millibars (mb) and weather forecasters use them on their maps. The pressure of the atmosphere at sea level is just over 1000 millibars.

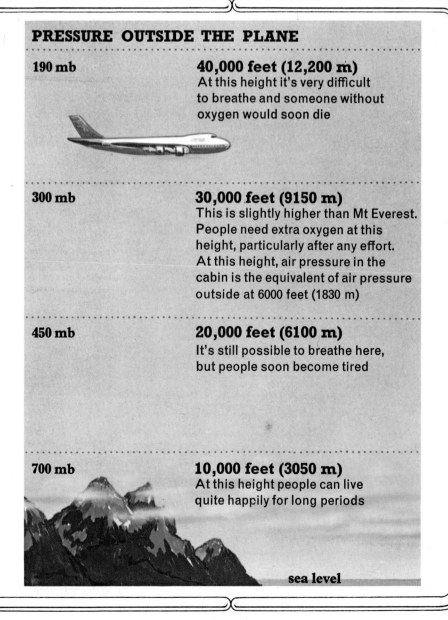

PRESSURE OUTSIDE THE PLANE

190 mb — **40,000 feet (12,200 m)**
At this height it's very difficult to breathe and someone without oxygen would soon die

300 mb — **30,000 feet (9150 m)**
This is slightly higher than Mt Everest. People need extra oxygen at this height, particularly after any effort. At this height, air pressure in the cabin is the equivalent of air pressure outside at 6000 feet (1830 m)

450 mb — **20,000 feet (6100 m)**
It's still possible to breathe here, but people soon become tired

700 mb — **10,000 feet (3050 m)**
At this height people can live quite happily for long periods

sea level

Meals are partially cooked before they come on the plane. The cabin crew completes the cooking in ovens in the galley. First-class passengers may get their meat or fish course specially cooked in microwave ovens.

Microwaves are good for heating organic materials—that is, things which were once living, such as fish. They can cook food thoroughly in minutes.

What's for dinner ?

With up to 350 passengers on a Jumbo, meals have to be prepared beforehand and stored in a freezer in the galley. Most meals are already on their serving trays, and passengers usually get a choice of meals. Special meals can be put on board—for vegetarians, dieters and diabetics, for example.

Reloading the projector

projector

Inflight movies

The movies are on extra-large reels of 16-mm wide film. This way one movie fits onto a single reel and can run without any attention. The movie reels are changed by ground staff before the flight. The projectors for the inflight movies are in the roof of the cabin. They have a mirror system so that only a small part of the projector sticks down into the cabin.

Looking through the window

The plane climbs up and up, passing through the clouds to enter a peaceful world of fluffy white, soft 'cotton', clear blue sky and bright sunlight. As it levels off, it is easy to forget that a rainy day may lie below.

Planes flying at 30,000 feet (9150 m) are above most of the really thick clouds that cause bad weather on the ground. Above the plane at this altitude, there may be a few *cirrus* type clouds—thin, streaky wisps that can often be seen from the ground. The air outside is very cold, but the passengers can enjoy the view of this sunny world that stretches as far as the eye can see from their windows.

Each type of cloud has a different name. Cumulus and nimbostratus are the ones that usually produce rain. The highest clouds are cirrus.

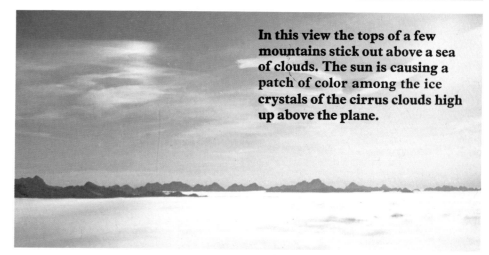

In this view the tops of a few mountains stick out above a sea of clouds. The sun is causing a patch of color among the ice crystals of the cirrus clouds high up above the plane.

There's a lot to see on the ground below as well as in the sky. If it's clear, the passengers can spot houses, streets and fields. This picture was taken from a height of 6000 feet (1830 m).

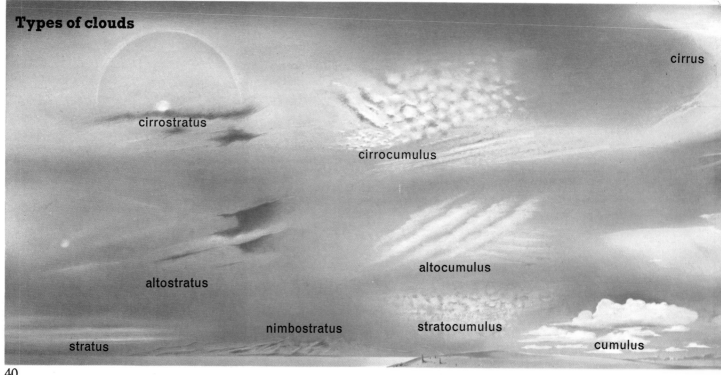

Types of clouds

cirrus

cirrostratus

cirrocumulus

altostratus

altocumulus

nimbostratus

stratocumulus

stratus

cumulus

Upper winds blowing against mountains rise over them in turbulent 'mountain waves'. This mixes up air of different temperatures which produces clouds—and sometimes bad flying conditions.

Water in the air

A cloud is made of millions of water droplets, like fog. This is why, when a plane flies through a cloud, the view goes misty for a while just as if fog has rolled in. These water droplets in fog or clouds are so small that they float on the air in the same way as fine particles of dust.

The droplets form from moisture in the air. Warm air holds more moisture than cold air, so the warmer air near the ground is usually free from mist. But higher up the air gets cooler, so the clouds begin to form. This is why clouds often have a flat base: below that level, the air is still too warm for the moisture to form droplets.

cumulonimbus (thunderstorm clouds: to be avoided)

The long descent

The end of the flight draws near and it's time for the plane to begin its long descent. At a busy time there may be several planes approaching the airport at once. To prevent accidents, the air traffic controllers 'stack' the incoming planes near a radio beacon, then take them from the bottom of the stack one by one.

Several air traffic controllers deal with the plane in turn. First, the controller in charge of the area bordering the airport looks after the plane's descent to the stack over the beacon.

Next, the Approach Controller takes over, bringing the plane down to a lower level as other planes leave the stack. When it's time for the plane to leave the stack, a Radar Director tells the pilot what course to take. The Director watches a radar screen and makes sure that the planes leave the stack at least three nautical miles (6 km) apart.

The approach

The usual way to approach an airport is to bring the plane in line with the runway, about 15 or 20 km (9 or 12 mi) away from it. Then the plane can pick up radio beams, called ILS beams, sent out from the runway.

The Approach Control room. This is at the airport, often in the control tower. The room is darkened so the controllers can see the screens.

On the Radar Director's screen each plane shows up as a cross with its number, height and destination. An instrument on the plane sends these details out automatically when it picks up the radar beam.

Area controller: 'Speedbird 501, you are cleared to Landmark to maintain Flight Level 330.'
The plane is already at 33,000 feet (10,000 m), called Flight Level 330 (always said 'three three zero'). This message tells the pilot that his present course is clear as far as the Landmark VOR beacon.
Area controller: 'You are cleared to descend to Flight Level 250. Advise when you leave.'
Pilot: 'Leaving Flight Level 330 for Flight Level 250.'
The pilot adjusts the controls and speed to give a smooth descent toward the beacon, rather than diving at once to 25,000 ft (7620 m).

11,000 feet (3350 m)

Area controller: 'You are further cleared to the Landmark holding pattern at Flight Level 110.'
The pilot joins the top of the holding pattern—the stack—at 11,000 feet (3350 m).

radial

1 minute

1 minute turn

4 minute total

In America, ATC tells the pilot to stack between two distances on a VOR radial

In the stack the pilot flies the plane up to the beacon, then turns and flies the opposite way for one minute. The plane turns again and heads back to the beacon. Every so often clearance is given to descend another thousand feet (305 m).

1000 feet (305 m)

VOR/DME beacon

Landmark VOR beacon

Radar Director: 'Turn left, heading 220 degrees to join ILS for runway 18 right.'
The pilot brings the plane onto the new heading which finally will line it up with the ILS beams from runway 18 right.

Approach Controller: 'Leave Landmark on heading 330 degrees, maintaining Flight Level 70, speed 170 knots.'
The pilot brings the plane onto the new heading, and reduces speed from about 210 knots (388 km/h) to 170 knots (314 km/h).

The invisible beam

The plane is now flying level, straight toward one end of an invisible path in the air. This slopes down toward the beginning of the runway itself.

Two radio beams sent out from transmitters by the runway mark out the path. These beams together make up the ILS or Instrument Landing System.

When the plane's instruments pick up the ILS beams, two markers on the artificial horizon move into view. Two other needles called Flight Director indicators also appear on the same instrument. These markers and needles show the pilot where the plane is in the ILS beams so that he can follow the beams down to the runway.

The Tower Controller in charge of the runway now takes over control of the approaching aircraft.

Automatic landing
Most planes these days have autoland equipment. Instead of the pilot having to make the corrections to keep the plane on the ILS beam, a computer on board does it. The pilot turns a dial to control the speed, down to about 135 knots at touchdown. The computer adjusts the throttles automatically. However, the pilot often flies the plane to touchdown, in order to keep in practice. The captain handles the plane and during approach handles the throttles.

Runway lights
Soon the runway lights come into view. Seen from the ground, the lights look rather confusing. But from the air, everything forms a pattern. Even if the runway is hidden by mist, the approach lights show the pilot where it begins.

runway

To get onto the ILS beams, the pilot flies the plane level until the needles on the Flight Director move. The pilot radios to the Radar Director: '*Established ILS for 18 right.*'
The Radar Director instructs the pilot to retune to the Tower Controller's radio channel.

The glide path beam (red) slopes upward into the sky. The plane's position in this beam is shown by the horizontal needle.

The beam (blue) that marks the center line of the runway is called the localizer. The vertical needle of the Flight Director shows whether the plane must turn left or right to get on this beam.

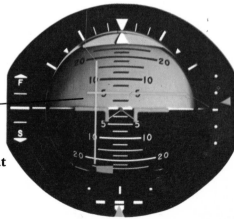

Flight Director needles appear on the artificial horizon dial

This dial shows the captain that he must climb to get onto the glide path and turn left to get in line with the localizer.

The Tower Controller, in the 'glasshouse' at the top of the Control Tower, makes sure that each plane has room to land. Since some planes leave more turbulence behind them than others, the planes must not be too close. If the runway is slippery or wet, the planes brake more gently when landing and need more time to get clear of the runway.

About 15 km (9 mi) from the runway, the pilot lowers the wheels and flaps to help slow the plane. The picture was taken less than 500 m (1640 ft) from the runway's end.

Coming in to land

It is always thrilling to watch planes landing on a busy runway. As one plane lands and roars to a halt, another one coming in looks as if it could easily collide with the one in front.

But the plane on the runway taxis off quickly and is well clear a minute or two later when the next aircraft screams in. If anything goes wrong on the runway, the Tower Controller tells the incoming plane to go around. At the decision height—usually about 200 ft (61 m)—the pilot must go around if the runway is not clearly in view.

If the pilot of the incoming plane has not been cleared to land by this decision height, or the runway is not visible, then the pilot instantly opens the throttles and pulls the control column back to overshoot the runway and climb to safety.

Touchdown

When the plane touches down, it is hurling toward the other end of the runway at about 135 knots (250 km/h). At this speed, the plane would get there in less than a minute.

As soon as the plane is on the ground, the pilot reverses the engine thrust. This helps to slow the plane down because now the engines try to push the plane backward instead of forward. The pilot applies the brakes on the wheels and the plane comes to a halt. The journey is over.

To make a VASI beam

You will need: a flashlight, thin cardboard, a pencil, thin white paper, a rubber band, a red pen, tape and scissors.

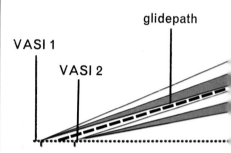

1. Roll the cardboard into a tube. Make the tube the same diameter as the flashlight and about three times as long as it is wide. Cover one end with thin white paper, secured with a rubber band. Color half the paper red.

2. Cover the other end of the tube with two pieces of cardboard. Leave a slot the width of a pencil.

3. Cut a band of thin cardboard 10 cm (4 in.) × 30 cm (12 in.). Cut a notch at both ends as shown.

4. Make two holes, one on each side of the tube so that the edge of the red, the slot and the holes are all in line. Push the pencil through the holes.

5. Bend up the ends of the band of cardboard to make a support for the tube and let the pencil rest in the notches.

shine the flashlight through the tube. Through the slot you'll find one half of the beam is red and the other half is white, depending on how high or low you are in the beam.

VASI

Visual Approach Slope Indicator (VASI) lights shine along the glide path as a guide to the pilot during approach. Each light has two narrow beams—one red, one white. If the plane is too low in the beams, the pilot sees both lights as red; if it is too high, both are seen as white. When the plane is exactly on the glide path, one is red and one is white. In the photograph above, you can see a red and a white VASI beam on either side of the runway lights.

pilot sees one red and one white beam when on this line

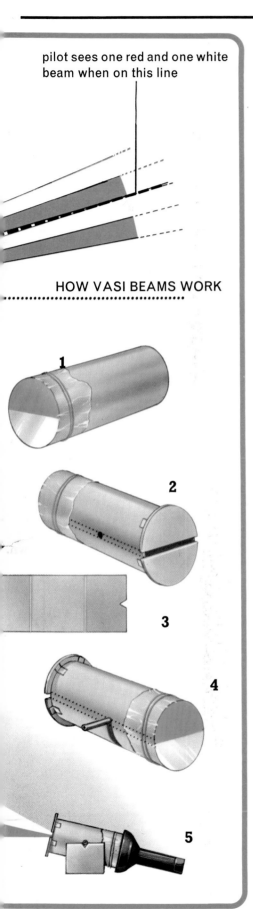

HOW VASI BEAMS WORK

1

2

3

4

5

The plane approaches the runway, nose down and losing height fast—about 5 m (16.4 ft) every two seconds. If it was losing height this fast at touchdown, it would hit the runway too hard. To prevent this, the pilot raises the plane's nose just before landing. The plane drops slower and sinks gently onto the runway.

Landing in a nose-up position is called 'flare out'. Watch a bird do the same thing!

The thrust—the engine blast—is reversed by a pair of metal shells which move over the back of the engine. These shells can only be seen on some planes such as 727s.

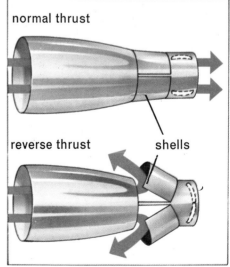

normal thrust

reverse thrust

shells

Berthing and baggage collection

Although airports the world over are similar, to many passengers the arrival airport is special—to some because they will explore new places and meet new people, to others because they're home or visiting friends or relatives.

The Ground Movement Controller radios which stand the plane must go to. The captain's job is not over until the plane is safely berthed. The huge Jumbo, 71 m (232.9 ft) by 60 m (196.8 ft), must stop on a precise spot. A signalman may wave the plane in, directing like a policeman. Or else there are lights that show the crew where the plane must stop.

As the plane comes to a halt, an engineer puts the blocks under the wheels and connects the ground power unit.

He plugs a microphone and earphones into a socket near the nosewheel to tell

The plane taxis in with its jets at low power. Each taxiway has a number and the pilot uses a map of the airport to find the way to the stand. If the pilot is new to the place, the Ground Movement Controller gives directions.

The signalman wears earmuffs to muffle jet noise. He directs the plane with large bats, brightly colored so they can be seen in poor visibility.

A wide variety of systems have been invented to guide pilots to the right spot when berthing. In this one, lights which work like mini VASIs on their side shine green along the centerline but red both sides. The pilot moves forward along the centerline until the strip light lines up with the aircraft type.

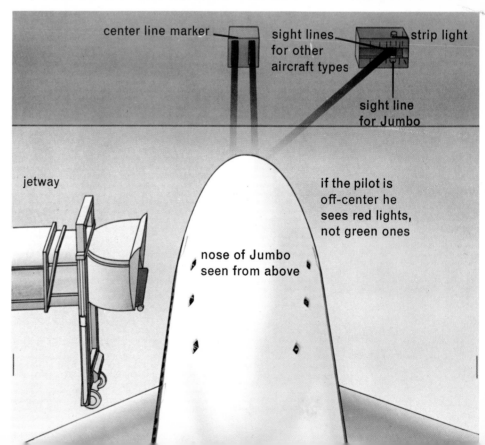

center line marker — sight lines for other aircraft types — strip light

sight line for Jumbo

jetway

if the pilot is off-center he sees red lights, not green ones

nose of Jumbo seen from above

the captain that the power is on and it's OK to shut down the engines.

The adventure is over

Within minutes the passengers are disembarking—perhaps onto a jetway that comes right up to the plane. At the same time, the baggage handlers are unloading the hold. They take the baggage to the arrival terminal where it is put on a baggage claim conveyor which takes it to the carousel. Passengers must pick out their own suitcases.

If it is an international flight, there's customs to go through. Then the passengers hurry off, eager to greet friends or business contacts, or to catch taxis or buses. But the airport carries on, buzzing with activity—other passengers and other flights ending or beginning their jet journeys.

The extending jetway has electric motors so an operator, standing at a control panel inside, can move it in any direction to suit the position of the plane's door.

Most baggage claim areas have a carousel system like this one at Dallas/Fort Worth airport in Texas. There is usually one carousel for each flight. The passengers may have to spot their own suitcases among hundreds of others.

Crash and fire services

Aircraft accidents are rare. Air travel is one of the safest forms of transportation in terms of numbers of people hurt for distance traveled. In 1977, figures show .387 accidents (.061 fatal accidents) per 100,000 landings.

Since the most dangerous times are during takeoff and landing, airports must be fully equipped to deal with an accident. Even if there is only a hint of trouble on an approaching plane, the accident services turn out.

Fire

Fuel leakage is the main danger. Any damage to the wings or engines may cause a fuel leak which could catch fire instantly and result in an explosion.

Speed is vital to fire fighters. Their vehicles are loaded with water and a special chemical to turn the water into a mass of thick foam. Foam smothers any fire by cutting off the supply of air. This starves the fire of oxygen and it dies

TO THE CREW, THIS 747 LANDING IS A ROUTINE EVENT, WITH NOTHING APPARENTLY WRONG. BUT AS THE WHEELS BEGIN TO TURN, A SHARP-EYED AIR TRAFFIC CONTROLLER, WATCHING WITH BINOCULARS, NOTICES.......

...THAT ONE OF THE WHEELS IS SMOKING!

THE CONTROL TOWER ALERTS THE FIRE SERVICES WHO ARRIVE AS THE PLANE COMES TO A HALT, ONE WHEEL ABLAZE. "IF WE DON'T HURRY, THE TIRES AND HYDRAULIC FLUID MAY CATCH FIRE!"

First on the scene are these high-speed fire engines, then the heavy-duty trucks as shown in the drawing above, especially designed to cross rough ground to reach a crash. The gun on the top sends a stream of foam over a range of 80 m (262 ft) or more, right into the heart of a fire.

quickly because things won't burn unless there is a supply of oxygen from the air.

Sliding to safety

In any emergency, when the plane comes to a halt the passengers must get out as quickly as possible. Today's big planes are so high off the ground that special chutes are used. The passengers scramble onto the chutes and slide to the ground. Leaving a plane in this way may be undignified and rough, but it's quick.

If there's a crash, it is important to know what caused it. If the crew were killed, the vital information about the last few minutes of the flight would be lost. So all passenger aircraft carry flight recorders which make a continuous recording of such things as the plane's height, engine power and so on. Flight recorders can survive disastrous crashes and the heat of blazing fires to yield clues about what went wrong.

This 'red egg' is the crashproof flight recorder. It continuously records about 90 different items of information, including the position of the controls and the direction of travel. It uses stainless steel wire instead of recording tape. There is enough wire for 25 hours of recording, and the same wire is used again and again, after first wiping off previous recordings.

AIR TRAFFIC CONTROL DIRECTS OTHER PLANES AWAY FROM THE RUNWAY.

"SPEEDBIRD 620 OVERSHOOT!"

PASSENGERS ESCAPE DOWN THE JUMBO'S TEN CHUTES AND ARE OUT WITHIN TWO MINUTES

TWENTY MINUTES LATER EVERYTHING IS SAFE AND THE PLANE IS TOWED AWAY

Dealing with the problems

Each wheel of a fully loaded Jumbo jet carries a weight of 22 tons, and an airport's runway has to support this weight plus the force of a landing. To bear this load, a runway has to be up to 75 cm (29.5 in.) thick.

Apart from being strong, a runway must also provide a nonskid surface. When a plane lands, its wheels aren't turning; they speed up to about 135 knots (250 km/h) almost instantly and then grip the runway as the plane brakes.

As the tires hit the runway, there's a screech and a cloud of smoke as a thin layer of rubber is torn from them and spread along the runway, leaving a black mark. When it rains, the combination of water and rubber buildup can make the surface very slippery and difficult for the plane's tires to grip. So runways have a special top surface to help the water drain off quickly.

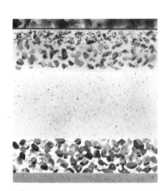

section of a runway

The top layer is strong yet porous so that water drains into it then runs to the sides. On runways with a concrete surface grooves drain water off.

Hazards on the runway

Inspectors regularly examine each runway for surface cracks and any dangerous debris. Many planes have panels which could fall off during the fierce vibration of takeoff or landing, and these must be picked up from the runway as soon as possible.

Another airport hazard comes from flocks of birds. A bird drawn into a jet engine at high speed can shatter a compressor blade, causing damage to the engine. One way to frighten birds away is to play recordings of the distress calls of birds at them.

Propellers save money
Propeller-driven planes use less fuel than jets. But ordinary propellers only work well at speeds up to about Mach 0.6, compared with Mach 0.8 for jets. Manufacturers are trying to make propellers that work well at higher speeds, and Lockheed has produced this design that may one day fly at jet speed using less fuel.

noisy approach routes into airports are often over cities

52

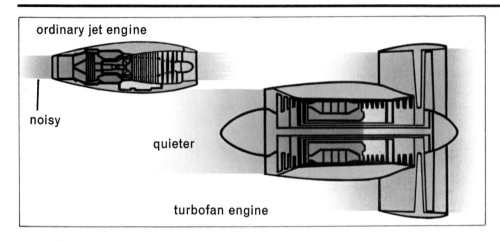

ordinary jet engine

noisy

quieter

turbofan engine

Cutting down on noise

Most jet noise comes from the high speed of the gas or air rushing from the back of the engine. The slower the gas speed, the less the noise. Turbofan engines are quieter than simple jets because the engine blast is slower, but they are just as powerful because they have a much bigger flow of air going through.

People who live near airports often protest at the noise. Authorities are concerned about the problem and are looking for ways to cut down the noise. But it is difficult to make jet planes really quiet. Noise can be kept down by restricting night flights and introducing wide-bodied jets which carry more passengers on fewer flights.

What next?

A few years ago, people welcomed the idea of cheaper and faster air travel. To keep up with the demand of more people wanting to fly, the number of jet flights were increased and then big jets like the Jumbo were built.

Concorde was designed for those who could afford the expense of the fastest possible passenger travel. Airports ex-panded and plans were made for new airports around big cities.

Today the picture has changed. Noise pollution and the scarcity of oil have made people wonder whether it's worth increasing the numbers of noisemakers and using lots of fuel to fly faster.

Replacing oil

What happens when oil supplies run out? By the end of this century, world supplies of oil will be getting scarce unless people stop using it up so quickly. But are there any alternatives to oil fuels such as kerosene for aircraft? Kerosene is a very concentrated way of storing energy. Batteries are far too heavy, while solar power would require huge collectors—about the size of a football field for a small plane. And imagine what would happen if the sun went in during takeoff!

Giant, nuclear-powered aircraft are possible but they could be highly dangerous, particularly if one crashed. Aircraft companies have also looked at different fuels such as liquid hydrogen and methane. These have to be kept very cold, but it seems possible to convert existing planes to run on them. It would be much simpler, though, to continue using kerosene as fuel. Scientists are trying to find cheap ways of making jet fuel out of plants, which contain the same atoms as kerosene (hydrogen and carbon) but arranged differently.

Engineers at London Heathrow use these mufflers for testing or warming up engines. The mufflers direct the roar upward, away from the buildings.

53

Supersonic flight

Before jet planes were used, a trip from London to New York by commercial aircraft took 13 hours. By ordinary jet, the journey now takes only seven hours —about half the time. But a new type of passenger plane flies faster still.

Twice as fast as sound, the Concorde jets across the Atlantic Ocean in just three hours—eat lunch in London and arrive in time for breakfast in New York on the same day!

When a plane gets close to the same speed as sound—about 1125 km/h (760.7 mph)—it has to be especially designed to cut through the air smoothly. To improve on normal passenger jet speeds (about 950 km/h or 590 mph) a new kind of plane—the Concorde—a supersonic transport, or SST, was made.

Hot wings

The Concorde flies up to Mach 2 (2150 km/h or 1339 mph)—faster than a rifle bullet. The rush of air outside the plane heats its surface by friction, just as rubbing your hands together quickly heats them. Even though the air temperature is well below freezing, the wings can get hot enough to fry an egg (though it would be rather difficult to do this!). The plane's outer skin is made of aluminum which withstands this temperature. (Frying pans are usually made of aluminum.)

Flying in the Concorde

The main difference between flying in the Concorde and other jets is that in the Concorde you get there quicker. The takeoff is faster and the plane climbs steeper than usual but, from inside, there's no impression that the plane speeds faster than any other jet. The flight is usually very smooth because the Concorde flies well above CAT and other air currents.

Out of the window you can see the horizon curving, though not as much as astronauts can. The sky is deep blue and the land below slips past rapidly.

The speed of sound

Sound waves in air behave like water waves. Drop a stone in water and watch the waves spread out. Now move a stick through the water. When the stick moves faster than the waves, it sets up a V-shaped wave like the bow wave of a boat.

A plane moving faster than sound sets up the same kind of wave in the air. When this air wave reaches the ground, people hear a 'sonic boom'—a sort of double thud coming from the sky. The noise comes from the air wave, not from the plane's engines.

The picture shows a model of the Concorde photographed in a wind tunnel to show the V-shaped air wave, normally invisible. A plane going at the speed of sound is said to be traveling at

Mach 1. The speed of sound varies with height. At sea level sound waves travel at 1225 km/h (760.7 mph). Ordinary jets are subsonic; they travel at about Mach 0.8. Speeds faster than sound are supersonic. Concorde has a Machmeter in the cabin to show the passengers how fast they are going.

Compared with wide-bodied jets, the Concorde is narrow, with only two seats either side. The windows are very small, as the Concorde flies higher than other passenger jets—up to 60,000 feet (18,300 m). The difference between inside and outside pressures means that the windows have to be small to reduce pressure loss if one of them should be broken.

As the Concorde is streamlined, it has a sharp nose which blocks the pilot's view of the runway during landing. This is why the nose 'droops' during takeoff and landing. During the flight the pilot raises the nose, which has heat-resisting glass to stand the high temperatures.

Build your own Concorde

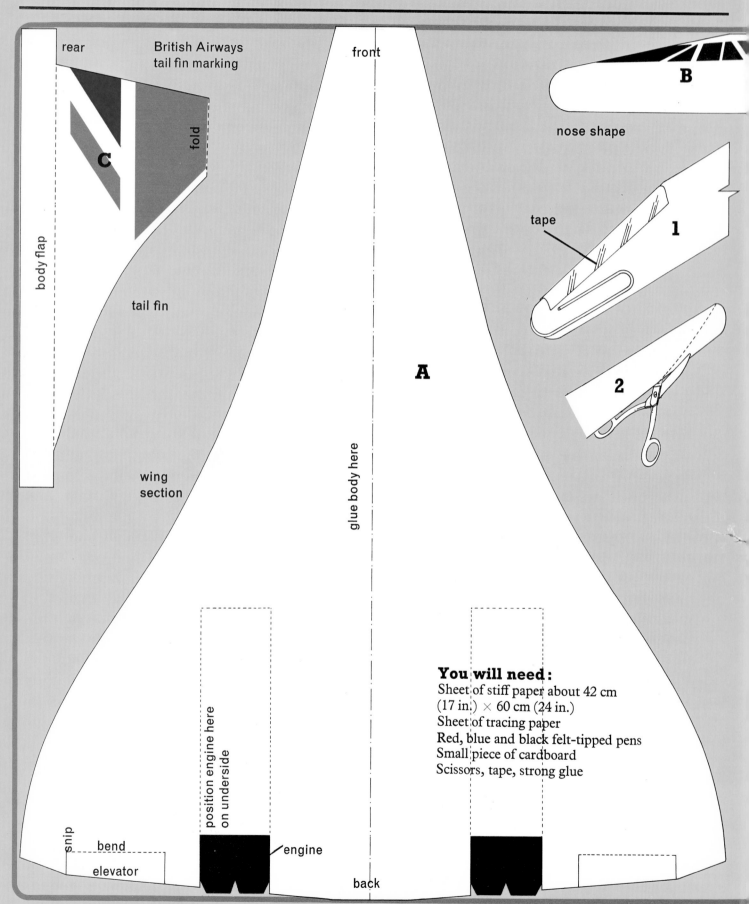

rear

British Airways
tail fin marking

front

fold

C

body flap

tail fin

wing
section

A

glue body here

nose shape

B

tape

1

2

position engine here
on underside

snip

bend

elevator

engine

back

You will need:
Sheet of stiff paper about 42 cm
(17 in.) × 60 cm (24 in.)
Sheet of tracing paper
Red, blue and black felt-tipped pens
Small piece of cardboard
Scissors, tape, strong glue

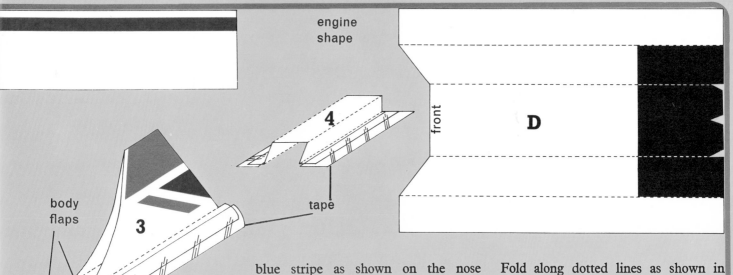

engine shape

front

D

4

tape

body flaps

3

Patterns
Trace off shapes A, B, C and D.

Wing sections
Cut wing section out of heavy paper using pattern A. Snip and bend elevators on rear edge of wing. Draw in engines with black felt-tipped pen on the top side of the wing.

Body
Cut a piece of the heavy paper 38 cm (15 in.) by 35 cm (14 in.). Roll it up diagonally to make a tube just over 2 cm (0.8 in.) wide. Bind it with tape around the center.

Nose
Cut nose shape out of cardboard using pattern B.
Push this inside one end of the body tube until the end of the nose is level with the end of the tube.
Pinch the tube against the nose and cut the tube to follow the nose shape. As shown in diagram 1, close the slit by taping the ends together, with the card shape inside.
Weight the nose end with a paper clip.

Windows
Draw on the cockpit windows and the blue stripe as shown on the nose pattern B. Continue the stripe and the cabin windows along both sides of the body as shown in the photograph on page 55.

Tail
Cut off the rear end of the body tube at the angle shown in diagram 2 and tape.

Assembling wings and body
Glue the underside of the body tube to the top side of the wing section, positioning the front end of the wing section 13 cm (5 in.) from the nose tip. You may need to reinforce it with tape to hold the wings in place while the glue dries.

Tail fin
Fold a piece of the heavy paper in two. Place the top of pattern C along the fold, trace off and cut out. Draw in your choice of airline tail fin markings on both sides. (Markings for other airlines are on page 60.)
Bend back the body flaps, then curl them around a pencil to give a curve similar to the body (see diagram 3).
Glue or tape body flaps to body tube so that the back of the tail fin is 6.5 cm (2.5 in.) behind the back of the wing.

The engines
Cut two engine shapes out of the heavy paper, using pattern D. Fill in black areas with felt-tipped pen.

Fold along dotted lines as shown in diagram 4 so the black part is outside. Diagram 4 shows one pair of engines folded. Turn the engine shapes over and glue or tape them under the black engine areas drawn on the top of the wing section.

Testing
Hold the rear of the body between finger and thumb at shoulder height. 'Push' model forward hard and level. A straight push will fly the model better than a curving one.
If the nose goes up sharply, add more paper clips until the model flies straight. To cure downward flight, bend the elevators on the back of the wing slightly upward.

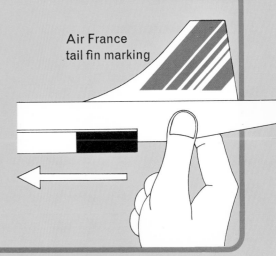

Air France tail fin marking

Plane facts

Jet lag

The world spins around once every 24 hours, rotating west to east. But even Jumbos can't fly as fast as the earth turns. So, if you fly from London to New York starting at 3pm, your watch will tell you that you have been in the air for 7 hours and that it is 10pm. You feel ready for bed, but in New York it is only 5pm and people are just getting home from work!

Can you work out what the arrival time would be if you left New York at 10am and flew back to London? (A clue—it will be 5 hours later in London than your watch says.)

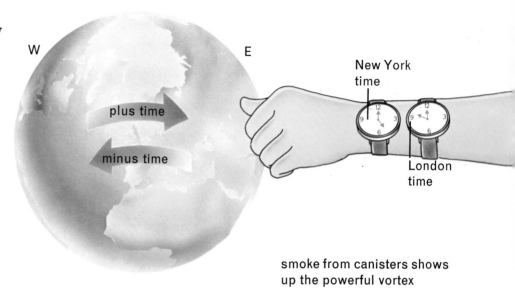

A powerful vortex

A Jumbo jet leaves a swirling wake after it in the air. This wake— called a vortex—can last for up to ten minutes and is powerful enough to flip a light aircraft over onto its back.

Vapor trails are formed from the steady stream of water vapor which is produced by the burning fuel in the engine. Heat from the engine stops the vapor condensing immediately into a fine white mist, so there is always a gap between the trails and the aircraft.

The Lockheed Starfighter, an early supersonic plane, had such sharp edges to its wings that they had to be covered with felt when the plane was on the ground to stop people injuring themselves.

A Jumbo jet is so big that the first flight, made by the Wright brothers in 1903, could have been made in the length of its passenger cabin.

smoke from canisters shows up the powerful vortex

Passengers looking out of a plane's window are sometimes alarmed to see the wings flapping. The wings are actually designed to be flexible so that the plane can ride through turbulence without damage. The wings of a Jumbo can bend up or down by up to 3 meters (9.8 ft).

There are 4½ million parts in a Jumbo jet.

A fully pressurized Jumbo jet contains 1.1 tons of air.

Cargo Jumbo being loaded

Cargo Jumbos

Some planes never carry passengers but are equipped for freight only. To make loading easier the nose of the plane opens up.

The idea of the jet engine is not new (squid have been using it for millions of years to propel themselves through the water). The first turbine—powered by steam, not gas—was designed by the Greek inventor, Hero of Alexandria, in the first century AD.

If all the rides taken by air travelers every year were distributed evenly among the world's population, everybody would have a trip of a little over 30 km (19 mi).

The top of the tail of a Jumbo is over 19 meters (62.3 ft) above the ground—as high as many modern five-story buildings.

Aircraft tires are filled with nitrogen, not air. This means that there is no oxygen in them so in an accident there is less chance of the tire catching fire.

Engine overhauls

A 747 may spend more than half its life in the air. When it is on the ground, engineers check it over and replace any parts that have reached a set number of flying hours. If an engine goes wrong, the plane is towed to a maintenance area and another engine put in its place. A plane only goes into the hangars once every year or so, when the whole structure is examined and overhauled.

Comet 4

Comet 4

The first passenger jet service across the Atlantic started in 1958 using a British Comet 4 aircraft. Some of these planes are still flying. This one, built in 1959, has now flown over 16 million km (10 million mi)—equal to nearly 400 times around the world!

servicing Rolls-Royce engines for a Jumbo

When an engine is taken off a plane's wing for servicing, blocks of concrete are put in its place to prevent the wing from warping.

Contributors

Our thanks go to the following for their help in preparing this book: Ron Wilson, John Cook, Brian Hampson, Linda Jones, Tom McGinnes, Roy Petford (British Airways); Jim Birchall (Civil Aviation Authority); Tony Lock (British Airports Authority); Ralph P. Magee (TWA).

Photographs

We are particularly grateful to KLM for all their help and co-operation.
Aerophoto Schiphol page 2. John Topham Picture Library 11. Steve Bicknell 23, 32, 34, 35, 37. Boeing 23, 39. Leslie Drennan 4. British Airports Authority (Gatwick) 21, 39, 50. British Airports Authority (Heathrow) 48. British Airways 21, 23, 25, 26, 46, 47, 54, 55. Austin Brown 40. Camera Press 39. Civil Aviation Authority 35, 42. D & K Urry/Bruce Coleman 47. Colour Library International 41. Dallas/Fort Worth Airport 11, 49. Dan-Air 59. S. Davell & Sons 51. Adrian Gray 10, 11. International Aeradio 20. IBM, United Kingdom 5. KLM 16, 22, 28-29, 30, 33, 42, 48. Lockheed IFC, 41, 52. Lufthansa 27. Archibald McLean, Marshall Cavendish 45. Ministry of Defence 54. NASA 17, 58. Picturepoint/London 3, 45. Plessey Radar 35. Qantas 24. Len Rhodes/Daily Telegraph Colour Library 52. Rolls-Royce 59. Robin Scagell 39, 40. Y. Aono/Transworld 24. ZEFA 10, 25, 49, 59.

Illustrations

Terry Pastor: Front cover. Rob Burns page 48. John Bishop 18-19. Tony Hannaford 2, 10, 19, 21, 25, 26-27, 29, 31, 35, 53, 58. Frank Kennard-14-15, 34, 36-37, 44. Trevor Lawrence 6-7, 16-17, 22, 28, 32, 38, 43, 44, 46-47, 54. Tom McArthur 40. Julia Osorno 12-13. Tom Stimpson/Ian Fleming Assoc. 4, 5, 8-9, 50-51. Trevor Vertigan 56-57.

QANTAS (Australia)

SABENA (Belgium)

FINNAIR (Finland)

AIR FRANCE (France)

LUFTHANSA (West Germany)

AIR CANADA

ALITALIA (Italy)

ROYAL DUTCH AIRLINES (Holland)

KLM

SCANDINAVIAN AIRLINES SYSTEM SAS

TWA TRANSWORLD AIRLINES (USA)

INDEX